SWORD
&
SORCERY

MILLER HALF-ORC SAGA

By

J. R. Marshall

DEDICATION

To my wife, Susan, whose patience, sometimes during antisocial hours, allowed the completion of this story, without hope of monetary gain.

To Mark Young, sitting on a beach sipping beer, reading yet another so-called 'final' version. He must have read the book ten times.

CONTENTS

PRELUDE...1

CHAPTER 1 3

CHAPTER 2 19

CHAPTER 3 29

CHAPTER 4 47

CHAPTER 5 62

CHAPTER 6 85

CHAPTER 7 98

CHAPTER 8 111

CHAPTER 9 124

CHAPTER 10 145

CHAPTER 11 158

CHAPTER 12 173

CHAPTER 13 191

CHAPTER 14 206

CHAPTER 15 226

CHAPTER 16 238

ACKNOWLEDGMENTS

Anglophenia: "How to swear like the British."
(Youtube)

Rollforfantasy.com/tools/map-creator.php

(Map Creation).

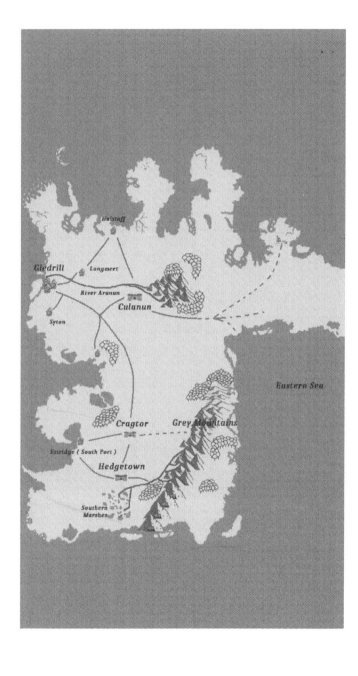

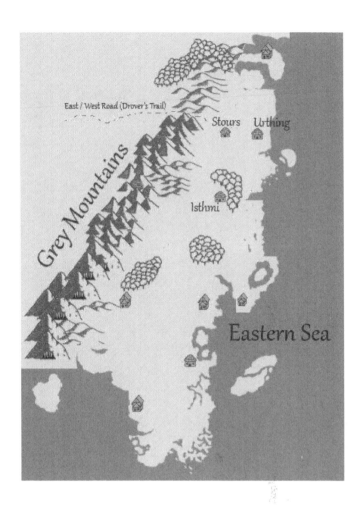

PRELUDE

Orcs are repugnant, typically filthy, usually brutal and often violent. Perhaps it's in their blood, a hereditary trait.

Living on the margins of society, they're generally less intelligent, shunned by those more capable and accordingly more affluent, but I've never met an orc who didn't know there was a better life to be had.

In the lands farthest from major towns, orcs will build houses, create communities, plant crops and keep animals, yet when that option is denied they live in forests or caves, securing any shelter they can find. It is these orcs that the townspeople see; orcs jealous of their neighbours' prosperity, orcs that steal, beg and frequently intimidate, occasionally raping or committing murder.

Most of the larger towns only suffer orcs to enter if they are slaves or specially approved, usually orcs are simply denied access. Yet despite their faults there are a few who are honest and hard-working and modestly clean, resenting the reputation that their larger majority have rightly engrained in the minds of other races.

CHAPTER 1

My mother was probably a whore, my father clearly an orc, and being abandoned quicker than a turd leaves the arse I was placed in an orphanage and later sold into indentured slavery. Certainly I was a disappointment as I clung to life with the stubborn tenacity of my bloodline.

Growing up with the dregs of unwanted children, no one championed any hopes of adoption, and whilst I was larger than my youthful years would suggest, and cleverer than anyone thought possible, I simply fought boys older than myself, until one day, aged eight, an unfamiliar face looked down at me, a stranger with bad breath, scratching the back of his head.

"I'll not pay for that, the ugly bastard's too much of a liability."

"The others are too young or already contracted," said the matron.

"But I'll end up feeding and training him; he'll be useless for a few years."

"Then come back in two years' time. He'll still be here, and besides, half a silver piece is naught." She knew Joe the Miller would have me working within the day.

I had a curious interest in this new development though the regimented life of the orphanage was all I'd known, now coming to an end as I became indentured, a standard contract of five years. A life of whips, chains, beatings and filth was about to begin.

Joe's farm milled grains for the production of beer, and was roughly three and a half miles south east of Gledrill, yet for all that it was a short distance, I had no perception of life outside the confines of the orphanage walls, itself situated in a poorer district of town.

Stepping out onto the muddy street, the cleanest I'd be for some five years, Joe played his last pretence of decent behaviour, ushering me onto a small flatbed cart pulled by a pony. I disappeared, never to see the town again except from afar, not until I had just turned thirteen.

Joe and his wife had a daughter, roughly a year older than me, and when we arrived I was paraded in front of them, told how to behave and obey, marched around the farm and locked in a cow shed for the first few days, that is until Joe managed to acquire some chains, manacles and padlocks to bind me.

Sometimes the most pious people are the cruellest, and although I started off willing to please, it became apparent that Joe had no morals other than he hoped the prayers of itinerant clerics would absolve him from calamity with the gods.

Yet there was one significant benefit. He always encouraged the clerics to spend time with me, an act of contrition, building goodwill with the gods by allowing me two hours a day studying, learning to read and write, languages, and anything the clerics wanted. Joe didn't want to know what I learned, or if indeed I learnt anything, he was simply buying grace, as he saw it, yet the clerics were enthralled.

It's not a boast to say I was a flattering pupil; the priests would leave jubilant, rejoicing in their own perceived teaching skills, for I never needed to learn a lesson more than once. Even though large parts of what the clerics taught was bollocks, I learnt quickly that knowledge was power, knowledge everything!

For years I worked on that farm, legs chained loosely, beaten and whipped into apparent subjection, yet never averting my gaze quite as fast as my master would have liked.

Now all vestiges of that miserable existence are behind, only friendship with Tam and Grimnir bind my heart, yet they are far away, west of the Grey Mountains. In the true sense of the word I am finally free, free to act without constraint, without bringing shame upon my two allies; these, the only two creatures I might under duress admit to caring for, who essentially rescued me from ruination and despair.

They were, *are*, good! Not obnoxiously, not like clerics spouting their religious drivel, but in some ways they were the best of priests, not trying too hard… just giving me a blessing!

Now in my old age as I sit upon my wooden throne, inlaid with silver and hewn from a mighty tree trunk, scribes sit on the floor writing my story, looking up at me as I scowl. Who will read it? My sons? They're as likely to burn the scrolls as appreciate the effort in creating a Kingdom.

Still, it's a vanity, my vanity; the story flatters me, of course it does, no one writes of their own incompetence… Scribes, ink upon their hands, carry on…

I am Miller, a half-orc bastard, a servant of none yet indebted to two individuals – a halfling and a dwarf – and as I sit under an elm tree the stars high above the tops of the forest start to appear, a gentle wind blows and I huddle around my fire, hoping it won't rain.

The darkness of my heart corrupts my mind. It's so easy to forget civilised behaviour, yet I'm not wholly ruined nor without redemption, nonetheless most of society treats me with contempt, accepting my silver yet seldom with cheer.

To humans I'm half an orc and to orcs I'm half human, that is to say not one or the other, blessed by neither, typically cursed by both.

Conflicted in thought, I watch my hound rummage through the undergrowth, and enquire of my spirit creature, 'Wisp', a dream companion who can sense the presence of creatures both under the ground and adjacent. Accordingly he knew we were some five miles from the group of humans we were tracking.

Wallowing in emotion, brooding introspectively, as

the warmth of this late spring day fails I watch the mist begin to gather across the forest floor, clinging to the ground slowly, rolling gently into the shallow folds of the land. A frost is forming and already the ground is hardening; a white sheen can be seen enveloping the tips of ferns and fallen leaves.

Berrek, an orc, the first of my servants, loyal out of fear, finished cleaning my armour and making the fire some hours before, and being an accomplished huntsman, his skill with the bow meant we ate well – the small doe shot earlier and roasted on our open fire is now half consumed. I'm tired, the weariness of the day catching up, yet as 'Git' my hound gnaws on a bone, I watch the twilight fail, waiting for the cold shadow of light to extinguish, for I revel in darkness and we will be breaking camp within the hour.

No sound out of place, the birds in the forest rest silent and nocturnal creatures replace those more accustomed to daytime activities. Looking at Berrek I ask Wisp to read his mind, for I need to know whether he will slit my throat. Having just killed his companions it is doubtful he is enamoured of me but I need loyalty and whilst fear is a start, trust will take longer.

"I need to meditate, Berrek." And I study his face, illuminated in the firelight, though both he and I can see in the darkness. Watching, I look for signs of deceit or treachery, and Wisp, my invisible companion, incorporeal, a spirit entity, reads his thoughts.

"You must guard me, for I'll be sat here for twenty minutes or so, unable to move." I speak softly for he is being tested.

'He doesn't understand.' Wisp spoke silently in my head. Across my consciousness I can hear Wisp's words as though listening to my own thoughts. *'But there's little malice towards you, he's uncertain what you mean.'*

Leaning back against the tree my hand pushes aside the fallen leaves and decaying vegetation, scratching the surface of the soil. Clearing away the undergrowth and closing my eyes, I lie still for fifteen minutes waiting, pensive, for Berrek to attack, but he doesn't.

Now with the first of my retainers sat opposite I take a chance, letting my mind drift, touching the earth imperceptibly with my left hand, meditating, falling into the earth song, the rhapsody of the earth's music, few can hear.

Down I'm drawn, oblivious to space and time, speeding across an ocean of altered perceptions, listening to beautiful sounds, my mind capable of the most magnificent imaginations, music playing in visual symphonies of colour, sound becoming combined with my senses so that I can hear colours as words, taste the music. The power of craft, the energy contained in the earth speaks to me, gently imploring to be gathered. I can sense how to fashion spells, joining parts that form an array, the intricate connective energies that when combined create the power needed to action my craft upon awakening.

Wisp reinforces my mental acuity, pointing out the snippets of power I need to gather, these strands of energy floating around me, and I can hear the deep voices in the bowels of the earth, the realm of spirit creatures and elementals.

Yet I do not venture too deep, for I am worried about my unprotected body, vulnerable to any treachery that Berrek might unleash.

Gathering with haste my powers of craft, the energy to fashion my spells, I draw my mind back, passing once more across the ocean of altered perceptions, the colours scintillating as they speed below, and coming to wakefulness and opening my eyes I observe Berrek, watching me as he lies on the ground casually poking the fire with a stick. He hasn't moved or threatened.

The energy gathered within, my powers as a sorcerer recharged, studying Berrek in his flea-ridden rags I know what Tam, my friend and mentor in spell-craft would have said had she known of the risk I had just taken. 'Never, ever leave yourself exposed to the elements, or in mortal danger.' She, my halfling friend, the greatest sorcerer I could ever imagine, she would have been wrathful.

*

"What is the most wealth you have ever possessed, Berrek?" I asked, for tonight I needed to encourage him and wanted to better understand his hopes and aspirations. I beckoned Git to my side, a click of my fingers, Git instantly obeying, curling up next to my knee.

"I never liked Grabbarzz's company, he was a tight-fisted bastard. He and Arkkzer never shared any spoils," Berrek spoke, as he squeezed a spot on his arm and sucked at a weeping sore that rightly needed tending with bandages and medicinal herbs, in jeopardy of festering badly. "Not that we ever got much coin. Occasionally I would have a few coppers, perhaps a half silver piece. But you killed them, and I'm alive." He touched the pitted sword that had belonged to his former leader, for I had allowed him to keep the best of their scant equipment.

Having a map of the small petty kingdoms that made up this land, I knew travelling into these local towns with a full orc would not be a problem. Towns in these parts were tiny in comparison to Gledrill, Cragtor or Hedgetown, places I was familiar with, being on the other side of the Grey Mountains that separated these two parts of a peninsula some two hundred and fifty miles wide. Tomorrow Berrek would be thinking his situation much improved, for tonight we were raiding a group of pilgrims, and they always had silver – always.

"Berrek," I growled, with projected brooding menace, "henceforth you will continue to call me 'Lord', as you do, but know that I have been called other names, 'Miller' by a few, but you will never address me other than 'Lord'. Do you understand?"

"Yes Lord." And he wondered why 'Miller', for it was not a name given to a warrior, although as I was half human he didn't really understand the logic humans used amongst themselves.

"You will obey me, always! And I accordingly will look after you, rescue you, vouch for you, but... and I want you to understand very clearly... the penalty for disobeying my orders is death!" I waited before adding, "Do you understand me?"

"I will not disobey you, Lord."

"You may defend yourself, but I forbid any killing

10

for any reason without my authority." I had probably laboured the point too much, but he needed to understand with certainty.

Whilst an indentured slave at eight hence my name, Miller, I had been given a human name at the orphanage. I'd never used it. Most of the time I had simply been called 'Turd', or other less complimentary expletives.

*

We passed through the woods, running where the trees parted, yet at other times moving with caution, stopping every mile or so allowing Wisp to descend into the earth and search for life within our immediate proximity. Berrek didn't know of Wisp's existence, and there was absolutely no need to explain that which was secret, but he was amazed when I said the pilgrims were camped one mile due east, and that they had established a fire and four out of five slept whilst one kept watch.

"How far is the nearest town?" I asked Berrek, as we progressed through the matted forest floor, "and tell me about it." Berrek, with a bow strapped to his back, dressed in a worn out leather jerkin with stained britches and oversized boots, smelt of shit and stood about five feet tall although he tended to slouch as he walked. He glanced in my direction.

"The town is about seven miles..." and he looked for the moon, judging the hour and pointing over my shoulder, "over there. It's mostly men, but there are orcs and inns, and..." he hesitated, "a couple of markets each week... but no one like you, Lord."

"Like me?" I asked. "What do you mean?" And he

stopped, staring at me and thinking carefully, choosing his words with slow deliberation, which I liked for it showed a degree of intelligence.

"Farmers, not warriors, and…" he sucked on his sore, "no one with your skill in sorcery." And looking at me, worried that he asked too much, he asked, "Can you heal me, Lord?" He crouched down in a submissive posture, head lowered, his gaze averted so he couldn't see my face, for he was subject and had never been shown any goodwill from his peers, expecting my wrath for his presumptuous request.

"I can, but I'll not waste magic on you." And watching as he heard the snub, I added, "But tonight I'll pay you such that you can secure the healing required. You'll be rich, if you obey."

"Thank you, Lord." But he had heard it all before and promises are easily broken, yet mine wouldn't be.

"How do you know they are pilgrims, Lord?" he asked. A good question, and I was hopeful for Berrek. By the gods I needed clever followers; Berrek might yet be useful.

"They pray a lot." And I said no more, but I wasn't certain they were pilgrims, it was just that Wisp had conveyed their dreams to me, and they sounded like the clerics that had plagued my youth, trying to fill my head with mindless drivel. Espousing platitudes about their wonderful deities, such that I was sure these pilgrims ahead were just that, pilgrims, pious morons, possibly evil, though gut wrenchingly familiar to me.

As we neared their camp, I enquired of Wisp to learn as much as he could. Wisp had during the earliest times of our bond been taught the concept of distance, and although distance was totally alien to a spirit entity, he had learned through associating with me to competently describe locations in a manner that I could comprehend. Now he imparted his knowledge that Berrek thought was magic.

Moving with stealth, my hound being told to 'stay' slid away to sulk in a bush, eyes watching as Berrek and I looked upon our quarry with neither of us speaking. We studied our victims, looking for any unexpected obstacles or hidden traps.

Before us lay a small encampment, a fire burning under an alder tree, two mules tethered some thirty feet away, visible under the firelight, whilst men slept sheltered against the rain by a small canopy similar to my tarpaulin that I had once possessed and lost during my passage through the mountains – a shelter against the elements, made of linen and wax.

Some forty feet away outside the fire's natural illumination sat a man with a lantern, a weasel-looking fellow passing his time scribbling in the dirt, moving twigs to and fro, a game he played to pass the time.

"Kill him," I whispered, and I watched as Berrek took an arrow from his quiver, nocking the end of the shaft, and took aim. The arrow was a crude, fat object, not like those purchased from skilled fletchers, yet I knew it was handmade and would run true, an instrument of death when wielded by my orc servant. I waited, quietly drawing my axe ready to charge if necessary and bring death to these sleeping, unsuspecting clerics.

There was a subdued 'twang' and a rush of air as the

arrow fled from Berrek's bow, flying swiftly, bringing death to its target, and as the watchman heard a sound unexpected, he started to react, but too late.

The arrow pierced flesh, pushing aside bone, embedding itself deep within the watchman's chest, knocking the man slightly back, gasping inaudibly, looking at the misery befallen upon his body. Staring in denial at the arrow he mouthed a sound but no warning was forthcoming, and shaking, he touched the instrument of his doom as he slumped backwards and sideways.

Even as I watched and waited perhaps a minute, I was sure that his spirit had not yet fled the body, the man coming to terms with the end of his life, lying in shock as I walked into the camp holding my two-handed axe in only one hand, allowing the directing of a spell with my spare arm should the need arise, ready to slaughter all bar one of the four sleeping priests, for I needed information and Berrek knew to keep one alive.

Standing over the sleeping pilgrim clerics, all men, I signalled for Berrek to kill three, drawing my finger across my throat, and pointing to the those nearest so that he understood, and my axe and Berrek's sword struck down, cutting the sleeping innocents.

Berrek was allowed to slaughter the third, who screamed as his first two companions lay dying, and with a modicum of skill skewed the third before he had chance to evade, using his new sword, thrusting the blade at the man's throat yet catching him in the eye, before stamping his right foot upon the cleric's neck, hacking down repeatedly as I sought to secure the last remaining man.

The fourth, awoken by the screams of his fellow travellers, cried out, scrambling on all fours, rolling and tumbling, imagining a wild animal attacked, perhaps a bear, and as for wild animals he wasn't far removed from truth. I kicked him violently in his left kidney, and he rolled over and coming to his senses, gaining a grip on his true position, turned to face me whilst all the time inching backwards, casting glances around, analysing his options, seeking an opportunity to flee. I gave him none.

Quaking, his voice constricted out of terror, he gave his name as 'Artorus'. He was about twenty-five years old, with shoulder-length hair tied back behind his head, fastened by a small silver toggle, and noticing the others also had silver toggles, though one had two, I presumed they were symbols of rank, perhaps devotion. His hands were smooth, and although a knife was fastened to his belt it was clear that he'd never done a day's work in his life. *Too busy kneeling before a stone altar, and babbling nonsense to a rock.*

Berrek bound the shaking and incontinent Artorus whilst I threw more wood on their fire, and after checking the mules I started searching through their possessions, placing sacks and saddle bags and all manner of equipment adjacent to the shelter. I wasn't rushing; Wisp had already informed me that there were no other humans, orcs, or goblins within a few miles, and the fire would keep most wild creatures at bay. We would be stopping here for the remainder of the night.

"Search the bodies," I told Berrek, and watching him search the first, I was pleased he practised this skill with competence, remembering my own initial inept attempt at searching corpses. I knew how easy it was to miss coins hidden in seams of clothing, or around the groin or hidden in hair and other filthy places.

Git was summoned with a whistle, and bounding through the undergrowth he approached, familiarising himself with the camp, sniffing at the dead men and getting in the way, such that Berrek kicked him aside, telling the animal to 'bugger off'. I was pleased that Berrek felt comfortable to swear and kick my hound, it showed he was becoming relaxed and I would study him some more, but not yet.

"Where have you buried your valuables?" I asked Artorus, and Berrek looked up, for he hadn't thought that treasure would be buried in a camp, and Artorus was loath to reveal the location, firstly denying the very idea and professing poverty.

"Excellent!" I exclaimed to Berrek. "It must be worth a king's ransom. Wouldn't you disclose a small stash, yet perhaps not a larger one?" I asked, and he watched and contemplated the point.

"I'll get him to talk if you want, Lord?" Berrek was examining a knife taken from one of the corpses, thinking it an improvement on his own rusty blade, and wondering if I would notice it missing.

Wisp entered Artorus's mind, examining his thoughts, ready for when I asked the key question; it was a trap, for whenever a person is asked a secret, even one they don't wish to reveal, their subconscious thoughts will flit across the answer, regardless of how determined they are not to disclose.

"Did you bury the stash, Artorus, or someone else?" And a moment later I knew the location, near where the watchman had been seated, an obvious place and I would have searched there in any event.

"There is no other wealth other than what you already have," lied Artorus, as I walked behind and reaching forward, slit his throat.

Blood gushed from his severed arteries, splaying outwards and away. I'd been drenched by blood before and didn't want the mess. He choked, coughing blood, rasping, trying to draw breath through his ruined trachea, and Berrek wondered why I had been so swift to kill and not question him further.

"Are you sure he had no more wealth?" asked Berrek, placing the dagger back down on the pile of plunder, thinking it wise not to steal, at least not yet.

"I know where it's hidden." And we walked over to the fallen watchman, whose dead, lifeless eyes stared up at the sky, and leaving Berrek to search the body, I walked nearby looking for disturbed earth, especially around the base of trees, and after ten minutes I found what I sought.

Moving dirt aside with my axe, and scraping away leaves, there buried loosely in the ground invisible to any casual glance was the main prize, a small chest wrapped in waxed cloth, made from polished acacia wood and beautifully fashioned with silver filigree.

Berrek looked up as I prised the box out of the ground; it was about eight inches long, seven inches high and five inches wide. He had stopped searching, not wanting to complete his present task, and it was obvious he was eager to share the spoils, but I told him to do the job properly, and bring everything he found to me.

Sitting by the fire I was studying the beautiful box, peering at the small keyhole and wondering whether Berrek had found the key during his searches, when he walked up.

"Go back and finish the job properly, you bloody greedy bastard!" I cursed at Berrek, who never having had any wealth had rushed searching the man, a job that rightly took twenty minutes, worried he would miss out on a bounty although none belonged to him. Greed had swiftly corrupted his mind, and rushing his task he had nigh on followed me back to the camp.

"Do it properly, you miserable shit, and oh, whilst you're searching look for a key." This revelation probably released some anxiety from him, for he now understood that I didn't have the means of opening the small chest, not that it mattered to the bastard, as I thought. He needed to understand his position; he would be lucky for any payment, yet payment he would receive – generous. *Berrek needs to know who provides. Not his wits but mine, nor his martial skills.*

CHAPTER 2

Far away at the mouth of the River Arunun, a barge draws nigh. Dock workers shout and haul on ropes, drawing the shallow river vessel closer, while gulls shriek, tossed upon the wind. A man stands at the stern, not venturing forward lest he dirty his cloak which is fastened tight around his body, a gold clasp at his throat. He looks ill at ease, impatient to disembark.

As the boat is hauled closer, water laps between the quay and the sides of the vessel threatening to splash upwards and this servant of the King steps back, knocking into the steersman, who begs the courtiers pardon, but no grace is forthcoming and manners count for nothing with this servant of nobility.

"Hurry, work harder, I've pressing business... Move, you bone-idle misfits."

Beckoning for his two servants to offload his baggage, he commands the dockers to greater effort, and swears at the tardiness of his men, who in truth are waiting for the gangplank to be secured.

Disembarking, striding onto firm ground he pushes a worker aside, looking both up and down the quay, glancing down a wharf, before grabbing a man by the arm and enquiring of an address.

"Tis shy of a mile, south west, on the edge of Gledrill, master," says the docker, looking at the courtier with a sneer, aware that there is little point in hoping for any appreciation or gratuity from the fop. *His sort are seldom gracious,* he thinks, and regrets not using the opportunity to misdirect.

"Go and fetch me suitable transport," the courtier commands, looking at one of his servants whilst he fidgets, disgusted by the stench of sweat, decomposing fish and the foul language uttered by the common men he finds himself uncomfortably in the company of.

Looking around, examining barrels as potential seats, kicking coiled rope aside and finding the least dirt-encrusted flat object, he draws a handkerchief from a hidden pocket and places it atop what he believes is the best of a bad lot, and waiting for his transport to arrive he cautiously seats himself, holding the sides of his cloak so that nothing drags on the ground.

He has a mission, scrolls to pass to Lady Tam Bluebottle, and she has secondary lodgings close to Gledrill though her main authority lies one hundred and fifty miles south, fifty leagues as the uncouth might say, and sitting there beside the docks, watching the normal activities that represent every harbour, he's glad he need not board another vessel, especially a seafaring craft.

After half an hour, there appears, creaking and rattling over the cobbles, a small cart drawn by two mules, a useful contraption given for the transport of light cargoes, and as the courtier's mouth opens ready to protest there follow four men bearing a litter, ahead of one nervous servant.

"It's the best I could find," the servant says, as he notices his master's frown.

"They better be good value and swift, for I'll need to return with them tomorrow afternoon." And walking towards the four men he notices his boot has become tarnished with a spot of tar, stuck to his sole. Almost imperceptibly the boot sticks to the stone cobbles with each step taken.

Reclining in the litter, he throws out one of his boots, closing the curtain, and commands he be taken to Lady Bluebottle's lodgings, whilst his servant collects the fallen boot and runs behind, scrubbing at the tar with his shirt sleeve and the corner of a rough woollen cloak.

Along the cobbled streets there are more soldiers than usual; preparations for war, guards securing provisions, requisitioning goods, paying a pittance or issuing promissory notes, and as he approaches Lady Bluebottle's residence, a collection of quality buildings, beautifully thatched, maintained to superb standards, he passes a column of wagons laden with goods, livestock tethered and led behind carts, sheep, goats, and chickens secured in cages, and a line of servants, all clean and prosperous.

"Pass me my boot, quickly," commands the courtier. "Hurry, we are nearly here."

And as the litter is lowered he steps out, flattening the creases in his clothes and cloak, examining his appearance as best he can. Raising his posture, he looks around, and spots a soldier examining and apparently admiring two fine-looking horses. A servant looks from the soldier to the newly arrived entourage and pocketing a few coins, walks over, smiling, and welcoming the courtier.

"Good day, sir!" he greets warmly, yet with a puzzled expression. "Forgive me, but I did not know we were expecting anyone?" Thrusting out his hand, he announces, "My name is Thrandar, servant to Lady Bluebottle," and looking the courtier directly in the eye, "may I be of assistance?"

*

Sifting through the spoils of a minor victory, Berrek, having thoroughly searched the watchman was cutting the heads off the corpses and stripping their bodies of any recognisable insignia.

A small pyre burned fifty feet from the encampment and he was resigned to his lot, understanding there would be no real wealth given him, for having been excited at the prospect of treasure, a first in his miserable life, he now knew nothing had changed. He would gain only a few scraps, a few copper pieces. Any hope of riches had slowly evaporated from his mind, he was once again despondent. Yet in this, he was in error.

The small key had eluded us, probably buried in the ground near the tent, therefore realising I would need to open the chest using magic, I decided to apportion the wealth, and Berrek, summoned from his duties knelt before me.

"Of the three knives you may choose one." And Berrek already knew the one he wanted. "Try these four pairs of boots and take the pair that fits you best, along with this belt and pack." As I cast the items in his direction, Berrek seemed cheered, a good start, better than he expected.

"Do you not need those other knives, master?"

"Lord!" I said, and he lowered his head and apologised. "These letters you cannot read, nor do you gain the contents of the box, but of the eleven silver pieces and six silver toggles, how much is fairly yours?" I asked, studying his response.

Berrek, unaccustomed to choice, especially where real silver is involved, scratched a flea away, rubbed his nose, and hesitantly opted for what he hoped might be achievable. "Two, Lord?" He didn't look me in the eye.

"Is that without the silver you've already stolen or with?" And Wisp had already flitted into his mind, understanding my questioning, enjoying our close association. Wisp thought these games were amusing, and I rebuked him, counselling that I needed to build an empire and no, I wouldn't be slaughtering Berrek. I think Wisp is slightly more wicked than I.

Not stolen a bloody strand, Wisp informed me and I was surprised.

"I've taken nothing, Lord." Thus spoke Berrek, apparently truthfully.

"Then," and I knew the danger of showing too much kindness, I said, "but you thought of it, I sensed your thievery."

"I did not steal!" And Berrek was right to defend himself.

The fire crackled and a very gentle wind blew some of the pyre's smoke towards us, before the wind, veering away, cast the stench adrift and I waited, knowing that I wanted to secure Berrek's loyalty. He was growing in my goodwill.

"The mules will be kept, but some of the miscellaneous equipment will be sold, along with the spare weapons," and considering the lessons taught by Lord Grimnir, a dwarven friend of mine, "they'll fetch six silver if we're lucky." I thought I was reasonably conservative. "Tent and provisions we'll keep, yet there's a cost for stabling and care of the mules."

"That makes twenty-one silver in total, plus twelve copper pieces, less costs," and waiting for the facts and reasonableness of my calculations to 'sink in', "maybe eighteen silver, approximate!"

"Take five now and when we leave town I'll give you three more, otherwise you'll drink and whore the lot." *Plus, it will keep him in my service,* I thought. "You will need to secure your healing in town and pay for lodgings." And he grinned, ecstatic, and kissed my boot. I threw five more copper pieces at him, a bonus.

"Don't get too pissed, or robbed, and bloody well behave."

The small town of Stours, is as Berrek rightly described a 'shit hole of depravity', full of orcs, half-orcs, men, all the scum of the earth, yet security prevails albeit a veneer. Scratch below the surface or walk unprepared down a side street, and woe betide the foolhardy.

There are groups of farms circling the burh, which is a small fortified town, yet houses and buildings spill out into the countryside surrounding the fortified interior, smallholdings scattered farthest from the centre. No one travels without weapons, even farmers, who have houses next to one another, their fields spreading outwards and away as spokes upon a cart wheel, the houses of each farm no farther apart than one hundred yards, a mutual protection, whilst their lands and fields form wedges away from each other.

Berrek and I packed up the makeshift shelters, waxed cloth secured to trees via rope. We didn't hurry as the sun approached midday, for we slept late. Git, my hound, ran free, chasing rabbits and deer, yet just before we broke camp he came running towards us chased by a boar, which veered away as it saw its quarry run between our legs.

"Bloody useless hound, your Git!" laughed Berrek and I found myself in agreement, as I essayed to kick the hound, cursing the animal's cowardice.

"We are to secure the stabling for the mules and you need to know where I'm lodging, before you piss off and whore," I said, but also thinking Berrek could do with a bloody good wash, not that my followers would likely emulate me in that regard.

"Will I not be lodging with you, Maste... Lord?" he asked.

"I'll know where you will be, and I need to be left alone for at least one day. Don't plan too much, expect to remain in town for no more than two days." And looking at Berrek, I asked, "Have you entered this town before?"

"Yes Lord, but only as a thief."

"Where's the most expensive inn?" I assumed Berrek wouldn't offer reliable counsel.

"There's three and a half places to stay. Well, maybe six if you include—"

"I don't, just explain the best."

"You're missing a trick, Lord. 'Shaleh's Rest' doesn't just perform services, but it's full of the finest rooms, although you'll be hearing me next door, and—"

"Do you think I want to live in stench and squalor listening to you humping a poxed troll? Just answer the bloody question."

"I think it's called 'Ferrex's', but I never got close enough, the security is too good, and—"

"Good." I shut him up, for I needed to think.

As we approached Stours, I once again ran my hand over the mules, looking for any branding, signs of ownership, for whilst I was sure the pilgrims hadn't travelled from here, I needed to avoid any dispute. There were no marks visible.

"Follow me before you disappear." And we approached between merchant buildings, hovels, brewing sheds, tanners, millers, and a whole plethora of stinking trades, stepping between gullies of excrement, blood and urine, a bullock led by a rope halter destined for the slaughterhouse.

A boy watched and whispered instructions to another, who no doubt thought my armour and equipment made me a good target for thievery.

"You." I pointed to the lad. "Come here, you miserable little shit."

"Why me, sir?" he enquired before walking over, cocky as an innocent child accused of the impossible, thinking he had an advantage, an opportunity to study me and give advice to his master.

"How would you like to earn a copper piece?" I asked, wondering if it was worth paying for the boy's local knowledge.

"I might like it, but three would be better." He was so confident for his age, only eight or so years old.

"Cocky little bastard," I said.

"Thank you, sir!" he grinned, looking down the side of my cloak.

And I smiled, wondering how long it would be before he tried to steal my purse.

I grabbed him by the back of the neck and lifted him off the ground, looking him in the eye, and Wisp was already reading his thoughts. "Who's your thieving master, boy?"

"Get off me you, you filthy orc," he said whilst wriggling, and looking around for support, he started screaming that I was trying to kill him.

"You tell 'Corrus' I'll have his guts fed to swine, if he comes near me." And I threw the boy to the ground, as he rolled away, swearing and threatening me with all manner of woes, yet quickly he quietened down, for I knew a name and he was uncertain. I was after all dressed as a warlord and perhaps his master and I had private business that he knew not.

CHAPTER 3

I approached Ferrex's, a collection of buildings built around a courtyard, and walking forwards, I was challenged by two half-orcs and a man, all looking enviously at my armour, and glancing at Berrek, they asked my business.

"Warrior, you may be welcome, can we help?"

"I need stabling, a secure private room, my clothing cleaned, a bath, two nights."

And thinking that there was no doubt I could afford it, they hesitated for my companion was filthy, looking dishevelled.

"Not him, just me." For I understood their thoughts even without Wisp's help. "Berrek, you can go, but get that arm of yours tended to." He grinned before walking away.

"I'll find you in two days, Lord!" he shouted back, his slight stoop so typical of many orcs.

Ferrex's place was indeed secure; the buildings faced inwards to a common courtyard with stabling on one side and as far as I could observe all external windows were secured with bars.

As I followed one of the half-orcs, he bade me wait a moment, beckoning for me to take a seat, though with my mail, axe and sword, I chose to stand whilst he went to fetch someone.

There was only one entrance that I could see, through the gated arch that I had walked through, and merchants and travellers spilled out of the common room, some casting glances in my direction, but for the most part I was ignored and looking back I could see the two remaining guards watching anyone who approached.

"Lord warrior!" came a slightly cheerful man, who having been informed of my arrival and told that I was addressed by Berrek as 'Lord', thought it prudent to carry on in like manner.

"I need your finest room – the most secure, bathing, my weapons, clothing and boots cleaned, the mules stabled and above all, decent food and to be left alone without disturbance, err, please."

It had become a habit when entering into an inn to exercise politeness or goodwill towards my host, it always seemed to help secure better service than misfortune might levy against my race, and today was no exception.

"The finest, Lord, is three silver a night, plus the other services will cost you an additional two, yet food is included, and ale half price." He looked at me expecting me to haggle, or choose something less expensive.

"I'll need to bathe first, but lead on. I'll change into my vest, and sit in the common room awaiting the preparations."

"Right! Err, follow me, Lord." And he led me down through the centre of the common area, my boots shod with iron striking the stone flags. So many times before had I entered thus, walking with purpose, men looking up and seeing a six-foot-four-inch half-orc with reasonably clean mail, a helm, war axe, and sword. They mostly averted their eyes, staring into their beer, looking elsewhere, hoping I wouldn't sit too close.

The hearth was surrounded by a group of merchants. *Always the same fat bastards stealing the warmth.* "I trust you will not be long in front of that fire, for I'll be back in ten minutes," I said, scowling as I followed my host.

The innkeeper led me to a ground-floor room, secured externally through two doors, each with bolts, and entering upon a large chamber, he proffered two keys. I was slightly underwhelmed, having paid too much for this room and experienced so much better in Gledrill. I was not impressed.

"Is this your best?"

"It is, Lord," said the innkeeper, slightly disappointed and defensive, though he had no right to be. Although the bed was raised off the ground, there was no pitcher of water, no tapestries upon the wall, no cloth drapes across the windows and although they were internally shuttered they looked shabby, and only one lamp hung from the ceiling, which when

I shook it, seemed to have scant oil left inside.

"It'll need refilling." Looking around, I asked, "Where are the arse wipes? I'll not be shitting in yonder bucket and using moss."

"I'll have them fetched for you, plus some more oil." Slightly chastened, he left me to undress, promising to collect the clothing when the cauldron was ready.

Crap! I thought. *I hope the food's better.*

As once before at the Haggard Hen, in Cragtor, I walked barefoot into the common area, two silver pieces, vellum letters and a knife in my hand, though I had locked the two doors of my chamber, and had cast a ward of protection around my backpack.

"My turn." As I pulled a chair closer to the fire, the merchants looking up thought it better not to protest as they made a little room, and farting, belching, and swearing under my breath, I flicked away a flea caught tightly between two fingers.

"Now then! You bastardised human." An orc pulled a chair and table towards me, as the merchants finally gave way, supplanted from their comfort, and looking up, I watched as an ugly brute, scars across his face, dressed in clothes I thought not his own, smiled as he slapped down a deck of cards and said he'd come to rob me of a few copper pieces.

"What if I don't want to play, or more accurately don't know how? And in any event, I might be poor, unable to afford your wager." I placed the vellum letters aside, planning to read them later.

"You wouldn't be staying here if you were as thick

and poor as you look," grinned the stranger, thrusting a hand in my direction, grabbing mine in an iron-like grip. "Flukaggrrr's, the name, slaughterer of thousands… I prefer ugly shits like you, soft half-humans who don't know how to fight," and he looks at me, my glowering menace, "or how to take a joke."

"So you can read?" he said. "Or are you planning to use them as arse wipes? Vellum can be cleaned and reused, you know. We can play for those if you're too poor, which I doubt."

"I might be visiting?" And I knew it was a stupid statement, wearing only a vest.

"Perhaps where you come from they dance naked in the woods eating mushrooms and fantasising over girls too beautiful for your ugly face?" said Flukaggrrr.

Studying this cheerful orc – a contradiction in terms, for orcs are usually taciturn, miserable pond life, treated with contempt because they mostly deserve their reputation; ignorant, uneducated peasants, uneducated because they are unteachable, not an unfair racial observation – I found myself pleasantly agreeable to his company.

"Do you want me to read them for you?" he asked, nodding at the letters, and I was amazed.

"You can read?" I asked, wondering whether he jested.

"Actually I'm not that good," he looked around for a girl or landlord, someone to refill his tankard, "but I can usually work out what three in four words mean, the rest I guess."

'Bloody hell!' I wanted to hire this orc. "What's

your business in these parts?" Wisp was already reading across his thoughts.

Flukaggrrr looked at me as he shuffled the cards, twenty-two in a pack as I later found out. "Just visiting, getting a few supplies." Without Wisp's report it was obvious he had more about him than he revealed.

"Teach me how to play, but I guess I'm only good for an hour. Unlike you I don't intend to stink for the rest of my life."

I took Flukaggrrr for two silver pieces and four copper, and that was despite his cheating, yet with Wisp telling me each and every card he had, it wasn't difficult.

In the end my bath was ready and I needed to spend the rest of the evening studying, lying on my mattress reading the letters and above all readying my craft, that is, the gathering of my sorcery. Meditating in the earth song, I hoped to reach out to Tam on the other side of the Grey Mountains, and I had yet to open the small chest.

"What's your name, human?" asked Flukaggrrr, as I bade him farewell. I already knew he would be here the coming day, and saying I wanted to see him again, for business would be good, he cursed.

"You're a cheating bastard human, but I can't see how you do it."

"No name. Just, Miller, but you can call me Lord." I knew it was pretentious.

*

I lay on the bed, studying the letters, badly written

in the common tongue, yet they spoke a little of what I knew. One of Edric's lieutenants, a sorcerer called Hjalmar, was in negotiations with a religious sect known as the Avarti, worshippers of a deity I knew nothing about, and this box was seemingly an offer of allegiance, of friendly association, possibly a ransom of sorts. Studying the letters, it was clear that Hjalmar was not too far distant from where I was lodging, located ten miles from the coast, perhaps some twenty miles southwards.

Tam had already informed me of Edric, a formidable sorcerer who was uniting barbarian tribes under his lordship far across the eastern sea, and that Culanun was threatened and almost certain to fall. It might take years but probably only months, for Culanun's rulership was capricious, the King vacillated, surrounded by weak and ineffective advisers.

Lying on the bed I studied the chest, feeling the weight, gently rattling and turning the box, trying to guess the contents. I knew I could open the box with craft, although I would firstly need to learn the spell.

So climbing off the bed, I sat on the ground and touched the dry, dusty flagstone floor, my mind preparing for meditation, and slowly I let my mind drift, falling into the earth song, rushing across an ocean of altered perceptions as I was drawn rapidly into the music, the rhapsody of sounds engulfing my mind, the beautiful songs of the earthen realm home to elementals and spirits, and others beside.

Wisp flew ahead, sometimes reinforcing my mental acuity, yet at other times enjoying his freedom and liberty as he sought out his peers.

The strands of connective energies that gave sorcerers their power tumbled past me as I delved deeper into meditation, the purple haze below where the spirit creatures dwell, drawing closer.

Descending, the earth's music changed, voices becoming clearer, and the strands gave way to the purple haze of the spirit realm, the connective energies disappearing above me as I sank lower.

Hovering in the midst of these tiny spirits, my mind reached out, calling a name, 'Sandy', the elemental companion of my former tutor and waiting, not daring to go too deep, the tiny entities gathered around, curious of Wisp and I.

However, not all powers in the earth are friendly; some of the greater powers who dwell yet deeper, resent trespass and a few are malicious, yet in the presence of these little spirits I was safe, and floating, buoyed up. Both by natural resistance and Wisp's support, I was able to revel in their association.

Across the hidden depths of altered time and space, my mind sought Tam, or Sandy, reaching out, imploring, distance twisted, not limited as a voice in the wilderness, hoping for any hint of their approach. I drifted enjoying the fabulous sounds, cascading music, visions flying across my consciousness. The most magnificent imaginations were conceivable as I pondered my craft, my mind revelling in incredibly complex equations for yet untested spells.

After a time unknown, possibly twenty minutes or several hours, I felt Sandy approach, sensing his arrival before he spoke, and like Wisp I could hear his thoughts as though my own.

His voice rumbling in my head, I could feel the warmth of companionship and goodwill that Sandy exuded. Whether it took an age or a minute, I knew not, but I gained an insight into events far away, of the preparations for war, and that many men were being recruited. Sandy feared there would be much blood poured upon the earth, yet not in Cragtor or Hedgetown, at least not yet.

"Gledrill will fall within the year, perhaps sooner, and Tam no longer has ownership nor possession of property in the city, so if you seek her, look to Cragtor and no farther."

"Will you enquire of Tam the danger of Hjalmar? For I wish to oppose him, and cause mischief in these parts. Does she counsel against?"

Many matters were discussed, yet much also withheld, and finally I asked Sandy to reappear in Stours the following day, around noon, for I had other plans in mind. Secretly his appearance would fulfil more than one purpose.

"If Tam agrees I will return, you'll know when I approach, but I cannot guarantee your request without leave to do so."

Surrounded by Sandy I was loath to say farewell, yet I needed to fashion my spells, and reluctantly rising above the small spirit creatures, Sandy's mind faded out of my hearing and with the help of Wisp I gathered the strands of connective energies that formed the components of my spells.

Gradually I brought my mind back, travelling once more across the ocean of altered perceptions, and opening my eyes, the room remained as before, yet hours had passed, no light filtered through the shuttered windows.

Although I felt both tired and hungry, and for all I knew it could be the early hours of the morning, not being able to secure a meal already paid for irked me. So still wearing my vest I once again ventured towards the common area and was relieved to hear voices ahead; perhaps Flukaggrrr might be present and I could find an alcove as is common with these establishments, allowing people to talk quietly, discreetly, conducting business privately without being observed, but as I entered the room, the area was half full, room enough not to worry.

Two hours before midnight, and I ate more than the landlord thought was fair, yet he should have known by my size, and in any event what was left over would only have gone to feed the servants. *They weren't paying.*

I wanted to leave a note for Flukaggrrr, but the landlord had no parchment or vellum available, or so he said, and despite Wisp suggesting I should cause him injury – a jest, or so I hoped – he was gently reminded that not all the world's a shit, and sometimes people don't have to obey my every desire.

In the end I thanked the landlord for the late supper, and with care and obvious seriousness, bade him pass a message to Flukaggrrr. "The orc I was playing cards with, by the fire? He may have accommodation here, I don't know for certain."

"Ah! He's dead! Or soon will be. Thank the gods I got payment from him." The landlord half smiled as he wiped the surface of his counter with a dirty rag. "I hope he doesn't owe you any money?" Reaching down to douse a mug in a barrel of ale, ready to serve another customer, he said, "The thieving swine was caught robbing a priest earlier, apparently he tore the cleric's ear from his head, and tortured the family, that is… until he was caught… or so I've been told."

The landlord disappeared for five minutes before coming back. Having thought about me, or so it seemed, he watched as I stood momentarily disbelieving that we referred to the same person, but the landlord seemed certain of his facts, describing Flukaggrrr's clothing and mannerisms.

"So what are his options for release? Can he pay blood money?"

"Really? How? By all the wickedness in the abyss how is he likely to be able to pay that?" And the landlord looked at me with caution, malice and suspicion replacing his neutral facial expressions.

"If you don't pay me… Lord, I'll have your mules and hound in compensation. Was he a friend of yours?"

"No, no he wasn't, yet I thought better of him; as orcs go, he seemed to have more about his character." And I wondered if this might yet prove an opportunity.

"Perhaps, aye, I know what you mean, yet he is what he is, or was, depending upon how swift the justice."

I was still somewhat disbelieving of the news, cursing Flukaggrrr's stupidity and my missed opportunity to hire him, but the innkeeper seemed sure of the facts.

"Landlord, wait, and I will settle my bill." Heading for my room, I opened my purse, containing approximately six hundred and thirty full silver pieces, divided between cheap gems, amber, silver whole, halves and quartered, a few copper, and a handful of clipped gold coins.

Returning to the common area, I laid out eight silver, and placed another two full silver pieces in front of him, saying, "I need to know everything... Half an hour of your time buys the first silver and the second depends upon what you tell me."

"Right!" He scraped the silver off the board, a wooden plank yet well crafted, and sweeping the coins underneath, he beckoned for his niece, an ugly squat girl, who through practised behaviour took the coins and disappeared into a private room behind the common area.

"Meg, get this warrior his equipment, and if it's too heavy ask Arg to help."

"Okay Lord, I can see you're an honourable... man." He chose his words with caution. "How may I earn the extra?" As he said this a customer approached, seeking three mugs of ale, and he bellowed for Meg to hurry. "Customers are waiting."

"You'll have to wait! Meg will be along soon," he said to the badly timed customer, and grasping a rag and rubbing his hands clean, we walked to an empty alcove, whilst he looking back making sure no mischief unfolded during his temporary absence, an absence that lasted hours.

I thought not to lie, yet not lying is not the same as disclosing every aspect of heart and soul, and the landlord was told that I was hiring men, that is to say orcs, half-orcs and the like, and that Flukaggrrr was possibly good recruitment material, and I needed to secure his release.

The landlord knew there was no advantage in warning me against thieves. *'Once a thief, always a thief.'* His words, given to me by Wisp, but irrelevant.

"How much?" I asked. "And 'I don't know' is not an answer." I looked at him, studying his face. "You'll get ten percent, double if it's less than twenty-five silver."

"Not enough," said the innkeeper, giving his name as Pudgeon, for he tired of being called by his trade title, 'Innkeeper'.

"Okay Pudgeon, you tell me?"

"A quarter silver a day is a good wage in these parts. I cannot see anything less than one hundred silver, that's a whole year's wage plus a little, but maybe more?" And thinking to himself he added, "It's a bloody fortune, for someone you scarcely know!"

It was indeed too much money, and I considered using spell-craft to secure Flukaggrrr's release, but there was an advantage in not doing so, a point Pudgeon need not know.

"So they would decline eighty silver and see the orc executed, or indeed forgo fifty silver?" I asked.

"I would," said Pudgeon, and I thought the same, yet that was not for me to decide, and reluctantly Pudgeon agreed.

"They'll still be awake, no one sleeps in that family

tonight, and the execution if it hasn't already happened," and Pudgeon conceded it probably hadn't, "will take place tomorrow before noon."

"Let's find out," I said. "At the very least they have a few hours before Flukaggrrr's death to think about their price." And watching, I noticed how professional in business Pudgeon was. No longer driven by morals, he sought to gain a reward, a commission, to profit from this miserable situation. He was wholly on board in trying to solve the conundrum.

"The crime is done," I said. "The payment is better than nothing. We may yet both gain from this situation." Pudgeon had already called for one of the stable lads to attend, who upon arriving was instructed to locate the injured cleric's lodgings and report back.

The price for Pudgeon's service was negotiated and we settled upon twenty percent below a blood payment of fifty silver, with a minimum commission of ten silver regardless; fifteen percent commission below ninety silver pieces and only three percent above ninety, for I was ready to walk away, sad, but not too poor, especially as I did not want Pudgeon complicit through laziness, or manipulating the blood price.

The family asked for three hundred silver pieces, and I informed them, "I will cheer the execution and keep my wealth, for a thief is only worth so much."

But in the late hours of the morning, I sent them my final offer. "Ninety-nine silver pieces, accept or remain miserable, content and satisfied that justice has been done."

Pudgeon tried very hard to get me to increase my offer, sure that he could compromise at something approaching one hundred and fifty, yet I was ready to give up, and as the condemned orc was led to his doom, the price was agreed, belatedly, at the last minute, so to speak – ninety-nine silver pieces, and I hated handing over the coin.

Flukaggrrr was brought chained and bound to Ferrex's, and Pudgeon initially resisted his presence, until I rightly informed him that half his customers were thieves, cutthroats, toerags and general criminals, and that he throve by offering a safe harbour in a town filled with the shit and scum of the earth.

Pudgeon received his ten silver pieces, a debatable amount for it was the minimum payment based on a blood price of under fifty, yet not the three percent that should have prevailed. Nonetheless, I've always treated innkeepers with courtesy, never knowing when I might need their goodwill.

By the time Flukaggrrr had been handed over it was approaching noon and I was concerned that I wasn't ready for Sandy's return. So Flukaggrrr was 'marched' to my chamber, still coming to terms with his narrow escape and silent, for he knew he was in my debt, and his obligations to me were yet unknown.

This was a show, a representation of power, of magical craft, and whilst Flukaggrrr was now a supplicant, I wanted to maximise the awe and any reverence I could secure.

Gone was his verve, the confidence he once had whilst playing cards, and I sat watching, waiting for Sandy to come, hoping that Tam allowed his arrival, hoping my oldest ally would acquiesce.

Half an hour passed and I studied Flukaggrrr, watched from the corner of my bed, thinking that more space might be required and so I told him to sit in the corner. I spoke a little more than he wanted to hear. Listening, he was terrified, for I told of magic and death, and how he was now my servant, bought for a price.

"You will call me 'Lord', and if ever you disobey me, know that the depths of the abyss await your wretched soul." I was dressed as a warrior lord, yet he was learning there was so much more.

Lying, I said, "I've summoned an ally, an elemental from the greatest depths of the earth. He'll be here shortly." For I sensed Sandy's approach, yet Sandy knew not my precise location.

I didn't call Sandy by name, protective of my former tutor, not wishing to reveal any information that might fall into the hands of Tam's enemies. Whilst Sandy wasn't the elemental's true name, it was not within my authority or purpose to give secrets away, regardless of how obscure.

Slowly as Sandy approached, Wisp went out to greet and inform him of my exact location, and waiting, I told Flukaggrrr that this was not his death, but to hold fast to courage, and as Sandy emerged, rising slowly from the ground, a massive spirit of the earth, an elemental, I could see the terror written across Flukaggrrr's face.

Sandy and I could understand one another without words, yet for me it was hard to hear in detail. The warmth of spirit, of goodwill, these were easy, yet words required concentration, that is until Sandy spoke, for all could then hear, even those behind walls and down passages.

This massive creature shaped roughly in the form of a man had an appearance of tumbling earth, rocks and scree sliding down a mountainside yet never reaching the floor, being replenished continuously. His form as though a phantom of the eye's imagination shifted ever so slightly, towering above us, head scraping the ceiling. He rumbled a greeting and the room shook.

"Few words," I cried, worried that his presence would shake the very foundations of the building apart, and Sandy loomed over me, casting a glance in the direction of the terrified Flukaggrrr.

"So…" He hesitated, and then I knew he spoke to Wisp, silently through telepathy. Wisp was being chastised, for Sandy was one of the most majestic spirits within this plane, the prime material plane on which I existed and the companion to my greatest friend.

Wisp and Sandy were both spirit creatures, yet their orders of magnitude were poles apart; Sandy good in nature, ancient and venerable, yet Wisp as a child, somewhat wicked. Yet to call either good or evil would be to misdirect, for there is no doubt I know how to be good, yet I choose, for the most part not to be. Nonetheless, Wisp was the closest in character to me, yet that did not prevent my 'love' of Sandy nor of Tam, his mistress.

If truth be told, I only had two real allies, people who were loyal and faithful regardless of opportunity

– my family, so to speak. In a world grown cold and grey only two were stalwarts regardless of circumstance – a dwarf and a halfling.

This spirit of the earth bowed his head, and I knew beyond doubt he wished me well, and as he spoke the room shook. I imagined the mayhem that occurred outside, panic in the common area and inner chambers of this establishment.

Falling silent, Sandy spoke across my conscious mind, passing on Tam's goodwill and counselling caution, for whilst I was more powerful than Hjalmar, Tam did not yet wish to oppose Edric, not yet, for she wanted to choose the time and place of a confrontation that was destined to occur.

So it was, as Sandy dwelt in my company, I was reminded that I was not wholly wicked, an obvious realisation but one I chose not to reflect upon, and I was given freedom to assault, pursuing action against Edric's lieutenant, but avoiding reference to any machinations from west of the mountains, that is Cragtor or Hedgetown. Many events were unfolding and Tam did not want to be drawn.

Touching Sandy, I thanked him for his presence, yet he knew, glancing once more at Flukaggrrr, that I began something monumental and my actions would save lives, though I never intended them to. He sank slowly into the earth; the flagstone floors lay undisturbed, no sign that he had ever entered the room, and I looked at Flukaggrrr.

CHAPTER 4

Thrandar holds his hand forward, looking straight at the stranger, yet despite his cheerful manners and grace, the recipient of this goodwill gesture ignores the token of friendship and instead glances around for someone more competent and agreeable, that is to say, someone more foppish, especially of a higher social standing.

Now to the readers, I, in my old age, as I recount this story, have to say there are few more disagreeable persons than Thrandar, but undeservedly and I regret using supportive language when referencing Thrandar, he is at least on this occasion fully within his rights to thump and strike this 'peasant', yet sadly he doesn't.

"I need accommodation suitable to my status, and an audience with your mistress, as soon as she agrees," he blankly informs Thrandar. "It seems a little quiet?"

"Err, I'm afraid the Lady Bluebottle is not here," mumbles Thrandar, somewhat taken aback by the visitor's manner, and wondering what his 'status' might actually be.

"No matter, I'll wait." He beckons for his baggage to be offloaded, and as his servants hurry to comply, Thrandar gives rather unfortunate news.

"Lady Bluebottle no longer owns the property," adding though needlessly, "she doesn't reside here," and as if to rub salt into the wound, "did you not know?"

The courtier stands there incredulous, apoplectic, demanding from Thrandar the reason for her absence, and Thrandar for one of the few times in his life comes to an accurate realisation that he doesn't need to fawn after a snob.

"So you are now unemployed and a waste of my time," says the visitor, as he commands that his bags be reloaded, and looking around his temper is not improved as the litter bearers have already departed having been paid by one of the servants.

The mules bray plaintively, as a wrathful emissary climbs next to the driver and flicking his fingers under the nose of the owner, commands to be taken to a suitable inn. "Something decent, not near the docks, nor peasants like you, somewhere worthy."

The driver seeks every undulation of the road, every pot-hole, as the slow cart with inadequately sprung seat trundles along causing as much discomfort and misery to its passenger as the driver can contrive.

Halfway through the journey, the driver stops, and looking at his ungracious companion, says, "That'll be nine copper pieces and one half silver to complete the journey."

Thrandar along with Tam's servants and livestock, provisions and suchlike have already departed; the courtier finds himself staring at a wretchedly small craft, wondering if he can possibly avoid his duty for he loathes his circumstance as he counts his silver, worried he might not have sufficient funds for a better vessel. Touching the gold clasp at his throat, he becomes reconciled to his misfortune.

His servants sleep near the bilge, in the bowels of the vessel, and whilst it's claustrophobic, the pitch of the sea is less grievous. Their master bunks with the captain; having secured passage he is resigned to his misery, yet it will get worse.

A week at sea and the vessel makes good time. Clinging close to the coast, their two-week journey is uneventful, unless you happen to be a courtier unused to the realities of the world, cushioned in comfort, with feather beds and fine flax blankets, servants to furnish breakfast each morning. Surrounded by polite society, he has wallowed in an unreal world yet now there is a realisation of how others pay his wage.

The twin-masted schooner yaws as it clears a headland, unable to reach each wave crest, leaning at twenty degrees. Straining to sail as close to the wind as skill allows, sailors heave on sheets, adjusting the twin jibs and trying to feather the mainsail for maximum efficiency. No reefing, all sails unfurled, the boat creaks and groans.

The courtier has long since given up trying to protect his fine cotton and silk cloak, now caked in salt carried upon the spray. The ship forges ahead whilst gulls gather on cliffs sheer to the ocean waves breaking and crashing below their cliffs.

How a man treats those beneath him says more about a person than any fancy words, thinks the captain as he smiles, the courtier retching over the side of the vessel looking decidedly ill. The master of the schooner knows that no one has died from seasickness.

"Tis a fine day, sir," says the ship's master, enjoying the sight of this worm vomiting, and wonders how long it will take for the courtier's stomach to be truly empty. Most of the time scarcely a dribble falls from his mouth, cast up and carried into the courtier's hair.

*

In Stours, Flukaggrrr grovelled, fearful and in awe, swearing an oath of loyalty, sweat dripping from his forehead yet the day was not warm.

"I need to hire men, half-orcs or clever orcs, and you, Flukaggrrr, will help me in that task." I watched him as he paid attention. "You know the area, and where to gain the fighters I need."

"If I walk these streets, Lord, I'll have a dagger in my back before the afternoon is over, yet I have eight followers fourteen miles away – five orcs and three goblins. I own a group of buildings, not large, nothing great, the former woodsmen were encouraged to vacate several months ago." And he spoke willingly. "Everything is now yours, Lord."

Goblins? I had no experience of the foul, vile creatures, other than I had killed some a few months before. "Like keeping cockroaches as pets?" I enquired.

"They're useful for basic duties. They understand orcish and some of the common tongue, no manners, usually treacherous and not particularly good fighters, yet they take instruction and I keep them from starving. The three have not betrayed me. I've trained them well, over the last eighteen months or so."

"Last time I met goblins, a hundred of the foul devils were trying to kill me." I remembered the time I had travelled down guarding a caravan between Cragtor and Hedgetown; the goblins had appeared from a wood and charged. "They ran away after I killed a few." Actually I had killed twenty-seven but didn't need to boast before Flukaggrrr.

"I really need men, or half-orcs. No more orcs, though I'll take your followers." And I told Flukaggrrr to go and get his possessions. "We will travel to the next town via your buildings."

Ten minutes later Flukaggrrr returned, and I was disappointed to see that he still wore no armour, his clothes were of a decent hard-wearing quality – leather britches, filthy cloth shirt and a sleeveless waistcoat made from well-tanned hide, a deep and broad belt, boots in need of waxing – but nothing different from the time he first introduced himself along with his pack of cards.

"No armour of any kind?" I asked, though I liked the scimitar that hung from his belt.

"Sorry Lord, I'm still waiting to find someone of my size." By that he meant steal from some suitably armoured individual.

I walked Flukaggrrr to where the mules were

stabled, and told him to go through the equipment and familiarise himself with my provisions. "Let me know of any items that whilst missing might need to be bought before we leave."

Git was reintroduced to me; baying loudly, he bounded forwards, glad to be reunited, Informing the innkeeper that I was still good for another night, "Though I'll be gone before the end of the day," I set off in search of Berrek and a whore house called 'Shaleh's Rest'.

Passing a blacksmith, I arranged for the six silver toggles to be hammered flat, before trading the various weapons and miscellaneous equipment stolen from the pilgrims for rations, two barrels of ale, cured ham and dried mutton, all to be delivered to Ferrex's.

"Sorry love," said a woman dressed in sheepskins, the fleece inwards, pressed for comfort, barefoot, a small silk belt wrapped tight around her waist. "No hounds allowed," she said, "but Mak here will look after him for you."

Shaleh's Rest occupied a narrow building, the front looking onto an earthen lane, yet they had added cobbles around the entrance and the whitewashed walls stood in contrast to the buildings nearby. The whole establishment seemed better quality than local buildings – new thatch on the roof, painted shutters, cheerful laughter along with drunken guests spilling onto the street.

"Come in," she beckoned, signalling for Mak to take the hound, who growled, hairs raised on his back as he shuffled slightly backwards behind my legs.

"Girl, I'm not here on business, I'm looking for

Berrek. Can you tell the ugly bastard that his Lord is outside?" *The miserable sod's probably poxed and impoverished, if not drunk to boot.*

"Who's Berrek?" she asked. "There's no one by that name here, though we don't normally ask for names."

"Berrek!" I shouted down the corridor, looking to step in.

"You heard the lady," threatened Mak, "not here."

"Bollocks!" As I pushed Mak and the girl aside, walking in as the girl fell over backwards, Git followed uncertain, lacking courage.

"Berrek," I bellowed again, "where are you? Get your miserable arse down here." Not expecting any trouble, confident and arrogant, I headed forwards as Mak drew a knife and pressed it against my back, touching the mail, making it difficult to follow through should he decide to wound.

Git, for the first time in his life did something useful, as he leapt at Mak's face, biting him on the cheek. Mak, who concentrating on his duty and the threat I posed, had ignored the hound and accordingly was caught off guard. Cursing, he swiped his knife downwards, trying to strike Git.

Wheeling around, I thumped Mak in the jaw, yet my axe scraped against the side of the narrow passageway, slowing my turn, causing my balance to falter and as Mak stumbled to the floor, landing on top of Git, who yelped, I also lost my balance, falling to one knee, crushing Mak's shoulder and left arm whilst Git, limping, scrambled away.

As both Mak and I struggled to rise, I muttered a three-second spell; twisted words, uttered across strained vocal cords that others listening thought a peculiar orcish curse, yet Mak was felled, stunned for a minute or two. Whilst my experience and strength enabled me to rise before him they did not protect against misfortune, and Mak managed to lunge at my boot before the spell was complete. The hidden greaves prevented anything more than a slight sting and the blade was twisted aside by hidden strips of metal sewn into the boot's leather.

"Sodding hell," I cursed as the girl started screaming uncontrollably, thinking Mak dead, and a murderous half-orc ready to kill her.

Deciding that I was causing too much trouble and knowing Mak wasn't dead, yet the whole town ready to descend upon me, I thought it better to withdraw and walk away. Though everyone either side of the street was watching, many with weapons, they were hesitant, calculating whether they wanted to confront a heavily armoured half-orc, replete in expensive chainmail.

Slowly, not running, as the screaming girl tried to close the door Mak started to come around, and turning to watch, I told the girl to get a grip. Wisp entered my head saying that Berrek was in a rear room and was getting dressed. *He's worried that he has lost something.*

I tarried in the street as Mak clambered to his feet, closing the door, and I could hear shouting and expletives uttered. People started to gather around as I slowly retreated, knowing that Berrek knew where I could be found, and that his name was probably not known or remembered.

Returning to Ferrex's, I bade the guards to expect an orc. "Berrek! You saw him when I first arrived," adding, "he'll probably be scratching his balls."

"Yes Lord, but…" And they were going to enquire more, but their brains didn't really understand.

"He has a disease!" Turning away, I said, "Allow him access to the mules, where Flukaggrrr is, but don't touch him."

The rations that I bought were assigned to Flukaggrrr, and saying I wasn't to be disturbed for an hour or so, I headed for my quarters. "We'll leave at dusk."

Locking the doors of my chamber and placing the chest on the floor, angled slightly aside in case I didn't like what was within, standing some twelve feet away I muttered words alien to this world, sounds and syllables tumbled from my mouth. This action of craft, an unlocking spell so many times practised, and as I watched, slowly the chest vibrated slightly, sliding across the floor, three inches forward and to the right. Metal could be heard grinding, followed by a click as a lock was sprung.

The lid widened slightly; imperceptibly a gap formed around the top and bottom of the chest and waiting, pensive, nothing untoward occurred, so poking with my sword carefully at an angle, worried the chest might yet be capable of harm, I prised the lid upwards. Nothing, no dart, no gas, no visible trap.

Now, I have an ability to see the aura of magic, a rare gift even for sorcerers, and staring, I couldn't see any sign of craft upon the chest. Nothing forewarned nor gave alarm, so cautiously I peered inside.

The chest was partitioned into three sections, each lined with different coloured silks, or so I imagined. Touching the material, it seemed beautifully knitted, as though spun and loomed by the tiniest of fingers. 'Silk' was a word I'd heard, but never having seen the like alongside wool, or flax, I guessed in ignorance, *This must be silk,* as I caressed the material.

The rear third seemed to contain a vellum folded letter, and the front section separated again in two, contained gems and a small golden key – not pure, for I twisted it gently between my fingers and it resisted corruption, true to its form, yet gold was certainly present, and examining the key I observed filigree silver inlay, beautifully crafted, embellishing this most functional of items.

The letter I lifted out, not reaching for the gems first, yet drawn to them nonetheless.

I confess that whilst I started to read the letter, a small rolled parchment fastened around with a ribbon, ends tethered by a small wax seal, I was drawn to the gems. Beautiful and exquisite, slightly opaque, there were eleven, and whilst my judgement was poor, they were certainly valuable.

"Bugger." I guessed somewhere between two hundred gold and a thousand; I needed to have them checked and there was nobody nearby that I knew. Perhaps Flukaggrrr, no point in asking the locals or Berrek.

As for the key, it looked the same as the chest, and I had no idea what it opened; perhaps the letter would reveal. I wanted to leave this wretched town and find the next, hire men, or half-orcs, at least twenty, maybe more.

It was one hour before dusk, several before midnight, and it had started raining, a slow drizzle. Entering the courtyard, I bade Pudgeon farewell, thanking him for his support as he greeted me warmly and wished every success upon my endeavours. I knew it was slightly disingenuous; he was glad to see my backside depart though his gates.

Too many stories filtered through this tiny town, too many strange circumstances surrounded my presence, and getting rid of Flukaggrrr and my filthy orc companion Berrek, was not an unwelcomed event, nonetheless from Pudgeon's perspective he had mixed feelings, my visit had after all been financially beneficial if a little scandalous.

Berrek stood there, dishevelled, filthy as usual, and poor.

"Someone stole my silver, but they let me stay the night," he said, as though to excuse his poverty.

"You were only there one night, you miserable bastard," I said, incredulous that he had achieved nothing and lost everything.

"Ah! You should have seen her, gorgeous…"

"Shut up, you ignorant turd," I interrupted and looking at him, wondered why they had let him stay. He was disgusting and I was in a conflicted mood, no longer charitable, yet there was a need to secure discipline, and Berrek had a weeping wound upon his arm, no money, and was still slightly drunk, plus Flukaggrrr needed to start setting standards.

Sod it!

"Pudgeon! I want a cold bath prepared, and a small tub to boil some clothes, his!" I ordered, pointing at Berrek. "Get your bloody clothes off, Berrek, Flukaggrrr! See it happens."

Berrek started to protest, but my ire was raised, and swearing I'd slaughter him on the spot, and sticking my dagger under his throat, "Lord," I said. "You call me Lord."

Berrek almost sobered up, and Pudgeon seeing both the benefit of four extra copper pieces and the need to get rid of my party, instructed a lad to see to my needs swiftly.

An hour later and a further seven coppers poorer – a wise woman had been summoned to tend Berrek's, weeping sore. I could have used some of Tam's salve that was hidden in my backpack but it was bloody expensive stuff, indeed I had a healing scroll that could also have been used. *Bugger that, I'll not be wasting valuable resources on a turd.*

Darkness had fallen before we headed for the gate. Berrek, whilst bandaged was cold; clothes and body were clean yet he had not the luxury of dry attire, and as we approached the gate, indeed there was only one, the mules laden down with our provisions, a militia man barred our exit.

"Open, we need to leave," spoke Flukaggrrr, his hair dank and wet, as were the mules, yet not I, for my waxed cloth cloak kept me dry despite anything the gods might throw at me.

Good. Flukaggrrr taking the lead, I thought.

"There's been talk of you causing trouble in town, some of the townsmen wish to talk to you," said the militia man who was joined by two others wearing hooded cloaks, similar to mine but not as large nor probably as fine a quality, though I couldn't be sure.

The first man held up a lantern, and approaching he looked behind to make sure his fellow guards were following him; he didn't want to be unsupported.

This internal perimeter was scarce more than a tall line of wooden stakes driven into the ground, with a dry earth ditch on the far side, crossed by a narrow bridge, yet what we saw was a gate about twelve feet wide, two leafed, with a wooden beam across the middle securing the two halves. A stake driven into the ground acted as a bar to keep the gates firm, and added strength against a concerted push.

I was so fed up with this wretched, flea-infested impoverished place, a wart on the backside of civilisation, that I played with the idea of gathering men in the next town and taking Stours for my own, securing a kingdom, carving out a string of fortified towns and villages, defeating one place after another, a beginning on my ambitions, and as I thought about it, the idea wasn't completely dismissed.

"Flukaggrrr and Berrek, if they don't open the bloody gate in one minute, you have my permission to kill them." I made my comment loud enough for all three men to hear.

And the approaching guard stopped, looking behind at the man to his immediate right, and inching back drew a dagger, as one of his fellow companions stepped three feet sideways and reached for a horn strapped to his belt.

"It's not wise to cause trouble," he said, "there'll be ten of us in no time at all."

"No there won't," and I bellowed a spell, ten words, one of the shortest acts of craft that I knew, developing a rage, lacking any mercy, determined to escape this backwater. My hand pointed at the man lifting the horn to his lips; a dart shot from my outstretched finger, appearing to enter his body, striking him in the stomach as the pent-up energy created two more magical missiles, each striking unerringly at the other two men.

Usually no singular dart created by craft will kill a full-grown human nor orc, although multiple strikes might, and as my skill in craft grew I was able to conjure three darts with each incantation. The missiles, almost silent, moved at the speed of lightning yet their range was less than a skilled archer might reach.

"Get down on your knees!" shouted Flukaggrrr, as the men reeled from the devastation upon their bodies, clutching chests and stomachs, wherever the darts had hit, and he ran towards the man with the horn, now fallen on the ground, lying in the dirt next to his shaking body. He needed no second instruction to submit, as Berrek ran towards the gate and heaved the crossbeam aloft, although he left the mules unattended.

Excellent, I thought, *they're starting to work with intelligence,* and I was even more determined to avoid idiots in my service.

Certainly we were observed; the cries of the men

struck by magic, the close proximity of houses and merchant buildings, all focussing my desire for haste. "No time to strip the men," I shouted, as Flukaggrrr pushed his man flat on the ground and grabbed the horn.

These gates were not the external perimeter of the town, so hastening forward we fled across the narrow bridge and without tarrying headed away as quickly as the mules could be encouraged.

CHAPTER 5

There were no paths into the wood yet for the most part the journey proved easy; the trees being deciduous and mature meant the undergrowth that hinders passage through younger woodland was mercifully absent. Most young saplings were eaten by deer or boar, the forest replete with woodland wildlife.

Great overhanging branches and broad-leafed trees gave some relief against the rain, but every so often Flukaggrrr would seek for the moon, a gap in the clouds, judging the time, or searching for the pole star, calculating direction, and there was smoke borne on the wind, gently blowing, diluted in the night-time breeze.

Flukaggrrr's camp, a collection of pig sties, sheep pens and wooden buildings, was surrounded and secured by a low stockade, a line of stakes not unlike Stours, but of lesser strength and height. The entrance was via a gate of boarded planks fastened together by twine and secured tight to internally protruding timbers, a removable barricade of sorts.

As we approached, some one hundred yards away, walking across a glade, Flukaggrrr cursed, "Where's the bloody watch?"

Berrek, laughed. "Perhaps they're humping the livestock," and grinning he swore he heard a pig squeal.

"Bloody useless! Sorry Lord, I'll have them grovelling in their filth before the night is spent." Nonetheless, dawn was nigh upon us, the slightest hint of grey light suggested that he'd better be quick.

"Open up, you ignorant bastards!" shouted Flukaggrrr.

After perhaps two minutes a goblin's head momentarily appeared, briefly visible before disappearing, trying to stay hidden yet observing who was outside.

There was a sound of scraping, and we watched as the barricade started inching back. A dirty hand angled around one corner, trying to pull the fortification backwards yet too weak to make much progress.

"Berrek, help me." As Flukaggrrr ran forwards and started lifting the gate, the goblin stumbled out as soon as the opening was wide enough, one hand missing and a dirty rag wrapped around his ruined stump.

"Get back here, you snivelling little toad," shouted an orc from within the stockade and the devastated, injured and probably dying goblin hobbled around the outside of the fence, looking at Flukaggrrr and then the rest of us.

Three dead or dying goblins – one impaled on a stake, another thrown onto the fire so that only white ashen bones remained, and the other crying in agony next to the same open fire. Flukaggrrr was wrathful and with Berrek's help had subdued one of the chief perpetrators of this mayhem.

Wisp was having a wonderful time, jumping between the minds of the five orcs and one remaining goblin, fascinated by their brutally corrupt minds.

"Berrek, search the buildings and check the livestock," I ordered, needing a base, a room to call my own, fed up with the rain and wanting to gain a degree of comfort. I also suspected that first light might improve my temper yet I so wanted to sleep. *Unlikely,* I thought.

Flukaggrrr's captured camp had tremendous promise, being hidden from any local town yet near enough with a full day's walk to obtain any supplies needed. The woodsmen had constructed living accommodation for ten families, well built, indeed the glade had been enlarged by the felling of trees used in the construction and all the buildings were sturdy, if not entirely watertight.

"What would you have me do, Lord?" asked Flukaggrrr, as he smashed his fist against the bound orc.

"Your men, Flukaggrrr, it's your job to keep discipline." And leaving Berrek to report to me, I looked at the injured goblin's arm, the hand cut off three inches above the wrist, bone sticking out. The bastard orc had forced the other goblins to hold the miserable creature down, whilst an axe had been swung repeatedly, all this revealed with the help of Wisp and my questioning. Although Flukaggrrr threatened the orc with torture, indeed all five orcs were questioned.

Taking Flukaggrrr aside, "What would you have done in my absence?" I asked, not needing guidance, but curious, wanting to better understand Flukaggrrr.

"I'd make him work like a slave for a week, then if at any time he resisted I'd kill him," and looking at the injured goblin, "at least that's probably what I would have done." After a pause he added, "But these orcs are your property now… sorry Lord."

"Don't be, and no they're not… Follow me." And I led Flukaggrrr into one of the least disgusting buildings. "He'll start here, I want it immaculate, and I'll have some of those unbroken sacks of straw used as thresh on the floor. This'll be my quarters, no one is allowed in here."

"He'll be worked hard! Bloody hard." Looking me in the eye, he asked, "Can the goblin be saved?"

Normally I would have said no, but Flukaggrrr needed to make the decision.

"I could use a type of salve that costs a fortune to replace, perhaps two hundred silver pieces," I said to Flukaggrrr.

I meant Tam's salve, a small pot of near magical cure stored in my backpack and carried across the Grey Mountains.

"Or, or I could use my magic that costs fifty silver

to replace." Meaning my healing scroll given to me months before by Grimnir, which could possibly be replicated in a large city for about what I'd said, but I wanted Flukaggrrr to understand and make the decision. Not weakness on my part, but he needed to understand the responsibilities and unpleasantness of greater command.

As a sorcerer I have no ability to heal the body; it is a significant limitation, although there are possible options that circumvent this restriction, but the alternatives take hours to prepare and don't always work. I had no desire to help the goblin anyway and Flukaggrrr knew a goblin's life was worthless.

"He needs to be put out of his misery," he said reluctantly. "I'll do it now." And drawing a knife he walked away.

During the coming days the camp was transformed; stores placed in one building, the livestock tended, shit piled in a corner, a full inventory taken, yet there was no parchment or quills to record exact figures so notches were carved on the door of the storehouse. I'd forgotten the small scrolls and parchment hidden at the bottom of my backpack.

I made the filthiest orcs wash their dirt-encrusted hands; it was as much as I could expect from them and I talked to Berrek and Flukaggrrr about my plans.

"I'm going away for a few days, and whilst I'm gone I want the following procured. A cart for provisions, harness for the mules, fresh straw and feed for the domesticated animals, bundled in bags or bales, enough for four months. Twenty barrels of beer, torches, lanterns, three gallons of oil."

And telling Berrek to leave me alone, I spoke with Flukaggrrr privately. "I intend to hire men, thirty or more. Everyone is to be as competent as Berrek, no less." And I impressed the point, "You will be in charge, Flukaggrrr."

Flukaggrrr listened. "I didn't ransom you because you were pretty, but because you were the brightest, most competent orc I'd met." Admittedly I hadn't met many. "You will decide who and when a person enters my employ, you will command in my name. I never want to see another stupid bastard under my authority."

And I reached in my backpack and handed him my purse, keeping all but one piece of amber and thirteen silver coins.

He stared at close to five hundred silver pieces, a wealth he'd never seen before.

"I will be back in about ten days. I'm travelling to a city, the far side of the mountains, about thirty-eight leagues, approximately." And Flukaggrrr looked shocked, wondering how it could be done. "When I return it will be with silver coin to hire the men I need. I intend to take Stours, a beginning." Flukaggrrr grinned.

"I'll give Berrek the three silver pieces I promised him, and henceforth everyone including the five orcs will start to receive a basic payment of a quarter piece of silver a day." Yet I knew that in time that would need to rise to a half.

"Use the coin for the provisions and try to hire two or three men, clever men... Upon my return you and they will be sent out to hire more."

Flukaggrrr watched me carefully, occasionally casting glances at the purse and wondering where he could hide it, knowing that he was trusted with a fortune and his life would be forfeit if anything went wrong.

"Flukaggrrr! After I leave you will secure this building; no one may enter, nothing is to be moved." And I placed my oil lamp in one corner, some other items in a second corner, and piled some thresh upon a third.

"When do you intend to leave, Lord?"

"In about five minutes." And I bellowed for Berrek, who came running. "Remember Flukaggrrr, as soon as I leave, the door is to be shut and secured. Neither you nor anyone else must enter."

"I'll secure it myself, Lord," he said.

Berrek appeared at the entrance and without asking walked in.

"Berrek! I'm leaving for a while. Flukaggrrr's in charge; make sure you support and obey him, and whilst I'm gone look after my hound." I handed him the three silver pieces I had promised. He stood there waiting for further instruction and I told him to bugger off and to do as he was told.

Flukaggrrr watched as I emptied some of my backpack, checking that I had all my equipment, and standing up. "You've seen some of my skill in spell-craft?" Yet not waiting for much of a reply nor worried by his sudden anxiety, I told him to leave in a minute, and secure the door as he had promised.

Before his eyes I uttered words unimaginably

difficult for him to pronounce; a few seconds later I vanished.

*

The mountain range grew in majesty the further south I looked, still, even at this more northerly location the peaks towered over me, foreboding, tipped with snow and home to wolves and other creatures.

Stood next to a cairn of rocks, the day fabulous, clear skies and a gentle breeze, yet cold as the wind blew down from the mountain range. The air was clear and had it not been for the sun warming the lands it would have been bitterly cold.

Walking towards the small pile of stones on a gentle slope, perhaps the remnants of an old grave three miles still on the eastern side, not far from a drover's trail, a mountain path that wound through the valleys now long since disused, I wondered who had lived here.

Time had flown, so much had happened during the last few weeks and gazing eastwards I was suddenly separated from a life unfolding, its potential as yet untapped.

Not so long past, I had tried the drover's trail, travelling from the far side, and having been driven back by wolves plus the need to look after my hound, although through the power of craft I had managed to complete the journey, albeit not at the first attempt. Now I needed to return to the far side.

Transporting myself could be done relatively safely up to my limit of four miles even if I had no idea of the terrain or location, but as Tam had taught previously, provided I knew the location and could visualise it in my mind accurately, the distances could be magnified many times over. You couldn't listen to someone describing a location and rely on accuracy, you needed to be able to visualise every detail, having a deep familiarity with the destination, although there were exceptions. Wisp could assist in some situations.

I knew this cairn for I'd been there before and having studied the area, it was immutable, ideal to travel to, not so a room in an inn where furniture might be moved or other landmarks that might prove too vague or transitory.

I'd witnessed Tam, my mentor, transport me more than a thousand miles to a distant continent, yet I could only dream of such power. I was simply a new-born infant compared to her. She was probably the most powerful practitioner of craft that I would ever meet; my tutor, my friend and ally.

With two applications of this craft left, hoping to only need one before I camped - I always tried to keep one charge back in case of emergency – Wisp was despatched to check upon a cave known to me on the western side of the mountains, and as he left my consciousness I waited uncomfortable, lonely having grown accustomed to the presence of my dream companion, or others around, even my hound.

The sun would shine for the next hour or so, though distant clouds threatened rain and sitting on the pile of stones I waited for Wisp's return, this slight hill giving good views across shrubs, ferns and gorse, along with trees not too far distant, about a mile away.

Sitting upon these rocks I wondered whose bones lay beneath my backside, what peoples had in ancient times inhabited this area, and looking around, I caught a grey flash, a blur, as a mountain lion leapt forward seeking the back of my neck, front legs splayed outwards, claws extended, mouth wide open revealing canine teeth as daggers ready to impale themselves upon my flesh.

Caught totally by surprise, the cat's body slammed into my back, knocking me onto the ground, claws scratching at my face and cheeks, although the helm gave some protection, likewise my pack proved an obstacle as the animal clung to my rear, its weight causing difficulty as I tried to rise and draw my knife.

The cat like a small boulder hindered my twisting as I essayed to dislodge the wild creature clawing at my head, pulling the helmet back and sideways, half digging into my scalp, for it so wanted to sink its teeth into me.

Struggling, seeking the straps to release my pack, I dropped my burden, discarding the weight, the animal claws sliding over my mail tearing my cloak as it along with the pack fell to the ground.

Crouching low, teeth bared, snarling with menace yet hesitant to pounce, wary of the dagger in my right hand, normally my sword arm but drawn quickly as I had started from a prone position.

With the element of surprise lost, it might have fled, it should have fled, for my size was massive in comparison. In fact, looking at it I thought it wasn't so large and was surprised just how much of a jolt it had given, but seeing blood on my cloak and dripping down one side of my face, it knew I had been wounded and was considering whether to press home its attack.

Switching my knife between hands, the cat watched my action, weighing its chance as I stepped forward, drawing my sword.

Hissing, growling, the sound changing in pitch and with courage lost it slunk away, moving sideways, turning once more to look at me as I advanced. I was wary of the concealment the undergrowth gave the animal as it disappeared out of sight, sliding between gorse and fern as silently as when it first struck.

Wisp returned only seconds later, and cursing my stupidity for not asking him to check the area for animals before he had departed, he enquired of my pain.

Blood poured down my face, my scalp felt tender and my cloak was rent in several places, cheek and jaw pierced in two locations yet I had more bad news, for Wisp said the cave I had hoped to transport to was occupied by a bear.

Shit. I wanted that cave. Having stayed before it was known to me, I could visualise it.

After a minute I decided upon another location, perilous, not fit for sleeping or meditating. Wisp had said the mountain lion was circling through the undergrowth some eighty yards away, not giving up, so with no good alternative I concentrated on my destination, a ledge upon a cliff which I knew very well, having studied and visited before. I ported myself, some thirteen miles, but the other side of the mountains.

Six feet wide, and eight feet long, a ledge halfway up a sheer cliff three hundred feet from the ground, the cliff a total height of five hundred feet with rocks strewn across the base, no way to climb down or up. The ledge was nigh near the middle, albeit flat, exposed to the wind, safe from anything that didn't fly.

This ledge was well known, as I had left one of my enemies, Krun, to die here. He was a thug and I suppose I murdered him, yet he deserved it having beaten me unconscious whilst I was chained and captive. I had brought him to die upon the ledge, yet in desperation he had tried to climb down as I knew he would, and falling to his death he had entertained me.

Still, it was a safe location although I wouldn't chance going to sleep. I still hoped to secure the cave and it was only just past midday, perhaps the bear might wander off. Wisp would be able to tell me and should that happen I would port myself inside, place a fire at the entrance and evict the animal for the next twenty hours or so. I was hopeful.

Wiping the blood off my hands and reaching into the backpack I sought Grimnir's healing scroll. The pain didn't particularly bother me but I was bleeding profusely and didn't particularly need any more scars upon my face. Already having one scar, it made it harder to shave, not least appearances count; a half-orc seeking goodwill from a stranger does better if he's not disfigured nor with missing hair, for gingerly touching my head I could feel loose skin – my scalp was torn.

This scroll, written unusually in the common tongue was straightforward; the energy was bound in the parchment and the words were like triggers, waypoints for an incantation that released the energy magically stored.

Most scrolls are written in arcana or elvish, yet someone had commissioned this scroll's creation and the intended recipient either didn't understand the usual languages or perhaps it was designed to be sold in one of the larger cities. Complex scrolls are always written in arcana for the language is designed for just such a purpose, allowing for more intricate subtleties.

Breaking the seal, I unrolled the parchment, keeping my head tilted to one side, for blood was dripping down, and even as I read the words contained therein, I wiped my eye on the side of my shoulder, the waxed cloak not helping very much. Nonetheless, as I read aloud I felt the energy from across the page, tingling at the edges of my fingers, words vanishing before my eyes, and uttering the final syllable of the last sentence, warmth spread into my hands and filtered throughout my body, tickling the tips of my toes and culminating at the crown of my head.

The bleeding stopped, and touching my scalp, I could feel no tear; the healing had been complete. There are of course magnitudes of healing scrolls, some more powerful than others, yet still this scroll seemed to have been sufficient for the task in hand.

"Can't you wake the bear and chase it out?" I spoke aloud, asking Wisp, already knowing he couldn't, but hoping he might have some special gift unbeknownst, for it was late spring and the sun wouldn't set until four hours before midnight, and if this bear was nocturnal as many of them are, I faced an uncertain long wait. It was at least five hours before dusk, I was getting fed-up waiting; either spend a cold night with torn cloak upon a windswept ledge or lie in relative comfort next to a warm fire and recharge my spells followed by sleep. The contrasts were stark.

'Nothing to be done,' said Wisp, speaking across my thoughts, *'but the animal seems nice and warm and content, although its dreams are very two dimensional, not much imagination.'*

"Fascinating, thanks for nothing," I mumbled, looking into the rain, the blood encrusted in my hair and upon my face being slowly washed away, little rivulets of water and blood trickling down my face and neck, absorbed into my vest, adding patina to my leather jerkin.

The sun set, and the cave only half a mile away remained occupied until two hours before midnight. I was soaked; a light drizzle was blowing across the mountainside. I was forlorn reconciled to my misery, when Wisp said the creature was awake and heading into the trees.

Waiting until the bear was at least a quarter of a mile away, a further hour, I sat cold for the damn creature ambled slowly, not appreciating my needs, and eventually getting fed up, deeming it safe, porting to the cave entrance, no risk of mishap.

It took me an hour to gather sufficient wood and establish a large fire in the cave entrance. I wanted no uncertainty with regard to the returning animal imagining itself able to enter.

Recharging my craft, I broke my meditation about an hour after midnight, and examined my cloak and pack, checking the extent of damage. It was clearly repairable with magic or by a seamstress but more wax would need to be applied.

It was about eighty miles to Cragtor, about twenty-six leagues, with no means of transport, for I had no waypoints to shorten the journey. Walking would take an age. I reckoned that with good terrain I could cover twenty-five miles each day, but this wouldn't be good, so maybe twenty, plus two portal spells, keeping one for emergencies. Twenty-eight miles, sleeping rough, though Wisp would forewarn of danger. Three days in the wilderness, trying to follow an old drover's road that over decades had nearly vanished.

In the end I set off at first light, using my first portal spell. I had three charged plus two magic darts, and passing the far side of a small wood, headed forward, the rising sun against my back, Wisp checking for animals and humans within a few miles' radius. There were a surprising number of creatures, and a dozen humans in most given locations, so in the end Wisp reduced his search area, concentrating on areas ahead.

The weather miserable, a cold wind blew across the moorland, birds seeking the sanctuary of their nests – mostly lapwing, curlew, grouse and other ground nesting varieties – not given to flight unless disturbed my approach, and finding the western trail midway through the first day I had lost it by the time evening came. So, entering a wood I sought a place to camp, the leaves and boughs overhead giving some relief from the weather. Huddled down under the leeward side of a giant oak tree, resting in a bowl shaped by the ball of spread roots, I settled for the night.

Lighting a fire in damp conditions requires skill

and knowledge, and I knew how to accomplish the task. Wood cut in sections with my axe, not a woodcutter's axe but sufficient for the task, were gathered around and stripped of their bark and using my knife I cut downwards on several logs, creating numerous feather cuts, curled strips of wood that increased the area where flames could gather. This with small amounts of kindling would suffice. Nonetheless, I was impatient and cheated, pouring a little lamp oil over the wood, and taking my tinderbox, flint and steel, along with a little charcloth, I huddled over my preparations.

Charcloth, half-burnt cloth, will catch a cold spark from the struck flint and when gently wrapped within the dry tinder could be blown gently until smoking, it would eventually catch a flame, enough to place underneath the oil-soaked wood. It took half an hour from starting the cuts to a fire successfully lit.

Awake much of the time, perhaps gaining two hours' sleep, Wisp would forewarn of wolves, and whilst they never encroached upon the fire, it kept me alert. Wolves will only attack humans if they're starving, and seeing the abundance of small mammals, rabbits and deer, I didn't worry too much.

A quarter of the way through the second day, Wisp advised that we were in an area devoid of wolves or men, so I recharged my craft, meditating and replenishing my portal spells, and thus covered a far greater distance than I had hoped to achieve, indeed by the second night I was only sixteen miles from Cragtor, yet there was more activity nearby. Looking across to the town, I could see the landscape change. Even in grey vision, the distance between my location and the beginning of farmland, an area that stretched some six miles from Cragtor's city walls, seemed deserted, yet Wisp told of many men hidden from sight, some trappers or huntsmen and others, possibly misfits in society, not finding the company of townsfolk agreeable, seeking solitude in the wilderness.

Tomorrow I would approach the gates before midday, using all my powers of craft to cover the distance, safe in the knowledge that security in Tam's domain was strong, and mercifully I would avoid an argument at the gates, for city gates close at dusk, and gaining access after dark is problematic.

Thus it was, I approached the gates two hours before noon, a queue of merchants and travellers, the usual activities of any city, and Cragtor whilst nominally classed as a town was large enough to be called a city.

Tired, in desperate need of a wash, wearing ripped clothes, in rusting chain mail, replete with ticks and lice, I waited in line not wanting any more grief, and walking towards a clerk, a man capable of checking cargoes and levying tax, I was ready to pay two copper pieces, the usual fee for non-merchants.

Had this been Hedgetown, there would have been no difficulties, for travelling down between the two places I had helped secure a caravan and fought hard against bandits seeking to waylay the merchants and steal their goods, and accordingly knew many of the soldiers. Entrance would have been easy, possibly free, but not so in Cragtor, knowing only one, albeit he was a captain seconded from Grimnir's men, yet not enamoured of me. Accordingly and unsurprisingly I was stopped.

"Whoa there! Not him." I had passed a silver coin to the clerk, who guarded by one of the soldiers was counting out my change, when another soldier approached, walking towards me, saying, "No orcs, even…" and sneering, "pretty orcs."

So bloody typical. It was the usual bullshit that I had experienced all my life, prejudice against my bloodline. At least this time I wasn't sat outside trying to gain access after dark.

Turning to stare at the ignorant sergeant, who was causing me trouble, he told me to piss off. "Orcs aren't allowed in here, you need to bugger off."

As the clerk was replacing my change, seeking my silver coin to return, the sergeant pushed me away, and for once I was too tired to protest. There were alternative options, and I just didn't want a fight. I was pissed off, yes, certainly, but the sun had finally come out, and I could wait.

"He's only stolen the silver and equipment," said the sergeant, looking at my bedraggled appearance, instructing the clerk to carry on. "We'll keep your stolen coin and return it to the rightful owner."

"Who would that be, your whore or wife, or one and the same?" I said, as turning away, the sergeant called for two of his associates to join him, in case I was more trouble.

Thieving bastard. He'll regret that. I smiled, knowing he made a serious mistake keeping my silver.

Retreating slowly, I walked through carts and travellers waiting their turn, and headed between two wooden sheds used as night-time shelter for travellers caught after hours, locked outside the gates, a protection against inclement weather until the morning, and sat down.

Wisp sought Sandy, who usually but not always stayed close to Tam unless sent on a mission, and deep within the spirit realm, news was relayed, Sandy found.

After a while, ten minutes perhaps, Wisp flickered once more into my conscious thoughts. *Tam knows.* It was enough. I smiled again, waiting a further fifteen minutes, and moved back from behind the wooden shed, approaching the gates knowing insufficient time had elapsed for a message to be received by the guards. I was going to be a nuisance and was looking to cause trouble, an entertainment for myself.

The sergeant, seeing me loitering summoned two armed men and approaching once more he drew his sword. "Piss off, you miserable turd, you're not coming in." And looking around making sure no one was in the way, he poked me with his sword, not to kill nor wound, but to humiliate.

"If I draw my sword, you'll be dead within the minute!" I played with him, watching and observing his confidence, reinforced by the other soldiers, one of whom circled around my side, forcing me to step back, not wishing to be flanked. "You stole my silver, I want it back."

"Bugger off before we take your pack and weapons." He whistled for the other soldier, the one next to the clerk, to join him, for he had indeed decided to relieve me of my weapons, worth more than he earned in a year, sure that no one would listen to a complaining orc, even a half-orc. He knew I was of mixed heritage.

Under no circumstance was I going to kill any of Tam's men, at least not in public, and I always chose not to infract upon her security. These men would be needed in the coming months, possibly years, for the defence of her lands.

So I parried, prolonging the confrontation, sufficient time for the message, which I was sure was not too far distant, to arrive.

Giving the sergeant and his men a lesson in martial skills, I spent ten or fifteen minutes playing with them. A crowd formed. I thumped, deflected, shoved, bruised and repeatedly knocked down the four soldiers who became increasingly aggressive as they failed to secure me.

What I didn't expect to see was a dwarven warlord sat on a grass knoll laughing and encouraging the soldiers to greater efforts.

"Bloody hell, Grimnir… stop encouraging them." I drove the pommel of my sword into the mouth of one of Tam's men, knocking him to the ground; less a tooth, I hoped. "They might get lucky."

One of the others, using his wits, backed off when I addressed Lord Grimnir without title, realising correctly, that there may be a mistake unfolding.

Of the two remaining, the sergeant belatedly retreated, cursing me, as the last one swung his blade in one final attempt, a sweeping action that left his body exposed.

So easily could I have skewered him, yet I smashed the flat of my blade against his arm, not necessarily breaking bones, yet disabling, his strength evaporating so he could no longer hold the weapon, his blade falling from his hand. He leapt back thinking himself in mortal danger.

Grimnir, rising to his feet, bellowed, "That's enough... Stand... No more fighting," and approaching, he cursed their incompetence, as I stowed my sword and picked up my pack.

Lord Grimnir, a dwarven warlord, the most formidable warrior I knew, my tutor in swordsmanship and the lord of Hedgetown, was a close friend and confidant of Tam. She, my instructor in craft, a friend, the finest most powerful sorcerer I could imagine. She was lady of this town, and he doubled as her steward when need arose.

These two, my only true allies, friends I would lay down my life for, these two stalwarts, the two people I respected above all others; and they were, I hoped, both here.

"Miller, can you not keep the peace for any length of time?" He laughed; he always laughed. "You're not even inside yet!"

"Lord! You warmongering bastard! I couldn't get in." And I glared at the sergeant, and said he owed me silver, before walking over, my height greater than his so I looked down upon him. "You would all have died, had I not been playing with you."

Gathering the soldiers around, Grimnir gave counsel that I should never be stopped from gaining access, day or night, and he emphasised night-time, to avoid any doubt, and I learned the sergeant's name. He was placed on a charge and demoted for ten weeks and tasked with digging ditches.

"You should have called for Glamdrun," said Grimnir. "He would have vouched for you."

"Who would have called for him? Not those bastards at the gates," I replied, looking at Grimnir. "It's alright for you, but I would have been ignored… at best."

I followed Grimnir into town; a soldier walked alongside, fending people away, for even in this prosperous city of Cragtor there were supplicants, people seeking a redress against wrongdoers, hoping to gain a brief audience with the dwarf.

"Better not be too informal, Miller, at least not until we're alone." And I understood, for Grimnir's ear could be reached through me, and I would be pestered to intercede on behalf of others, fawned upon, pursued by sycophants.

"Are you here for long?" I asked, hoping to spend some time in his company. So many questions to ask, so much information and counsel to glean.

"I'm riding down to Hedgetown tomorrow, you can join me if you like. It'll just be me and two men, no caravan this time."

"Can I see you and Tam tonight?" I asked, hoping he would agree, impatient, keen to renew the friendship.

"I'm good, but can't speak for Tam, she'll let you know. Where are you staying? Best not this castle, unless you're poor," and looking at me, examining my filth and torn cloak, "are you?"

"No! I'll seek lodgings at the Hen." I meant the

'Haggard Hen', a place well known and offering decent service.

"Best bow and grovel a bit," said Grimnir. "People are watching you."

I bent down, head lowered, nodding like an imbecile, and Grimnir gestured dismissively in my direction, turned his back and walked away.

CHAPTER 6

The 'Hen' was a superior inn, capable of offering services other less expensive places couldn't or had no call for, that is to say: cleaning of clothes, bathing, scrubbing of mail, decent food, secure quality lodging, and less trouble.

But I was flea ridden, and looked a mess, and approaching the inn, there were the usual fops, dandies and wealthy merchants outside, not barring my entrance, but scowling and observing my approach. I needed the innkeeper to come outside, needing his ministrations, and I asked three people outside to fetch the landlord.

Two begrudgingly complied, entering under a low arched doorway, no doubt to tease the owner that he had an orc outside, asking for a free room. And as the innkeeper emerged to see the beggar off, he laughed and looking at me said, "You can look quite presentable, Master Miller," and rubbing his chin, smiling, "but not today, apparently."

Watching a large cauldron of water warming over a fire, I had taken my clothes off and stood naked; my spare vest had been left at Flukaggrrr's camp.

Staff had taken my mail away to be scrubbed with cloth and sand, my leather jerkin to be scraped and cleaned, my other clothes piled in a heap ready to be boil washed.

A stable lad dragged a large metal tub across the cobbled courtyard, helped by one hand of the innkeeper, his other holding a threadbare vest, "The largest I could find, master warrior," and mercifully it was large enough, and clean.

"This cloak can be repaired but needs cleaning and re-waxing, return it to my quarters when done." I dropped it in front of the boy who, looking, said his mother could do the job of cleaning, waxing and repair if I wanted her to. He looked at the innkeeper, his master, for approval.

"I don't have your old room, but I've space in the dormitory, or a choice of two of the best rooms." Yet remembering the overpriced chamber in Stours, I ask to be shown both.

"How much?" I asked as I looked at the first of the best, above the innkeeper's own lodging, not ideal for me, for I needed to be on the ground floor.

"Three and a half silver a night, but food and beer is free, as always."

"And the other services? Mail, cleaning etc.," I asked, thinking I still needed to be on the ground floor.

"One silver should be enough, but perhaps seven copper more depending upon your cloak."

"Your price is agreed, and I will pay it, but I need my old room. Can you swap us around? It'll only be one night, surely he won't mind a better room for this evening?"

The innkeeper had never had a guest forego a better room for the same cost, so he thought about it and said he would let me know. In the end the other occupant had no choice, the innkeeper simply told him to move, and with a little clean thresh across the floor, I was installed on the ground floor.

A mattress in one corner, arse wipes on a shelf by the door, shutters across the window, I balanced my helm on the closed leaves of the shuttered window, a precaution in case a thief tried to gain access. Spiking the door closed with my knife, I sat down on the floor, scraping the thresh aside, my hand touching the ground, and fell into meditation.

Recharged having gathered the connective energies and passing back across the ocean of altered perceptions, I resurfaced after only an hour or so. There had been no echo of Sandy, nor had I noticed eddies in the connective energies suggesting other sorcerers were harvesting their spell-craft, yet I knew the water in the cauldron would have been poured into my bathing tub, the remainder used to boil clothes.

An hour later, clean yet still wearing the vest, for my clothes were drying, I sat adjacent to the fire. A board, a platter of assorted quartered pies and sausages, along with a pitcher of beer, took up most of the room on a small table alongside.

Outside my vest, jerkin, britches and leggings were drying in the wind, yet being attended by a boy, who was turning my boots as they were propped up by the cauldron's fire; turning them every five minutes, for he was tasked with applying oils to the leather, but the boots were not yet free from moisture. It would take three hours before matters were finished, already my mail had been scrubbed clean, and the same oil would be lightly coated over the metal in due course.

Still as I sat there, nodding off, the weariness of travel catching up, the food and ale relaxing, so soporific, I caught myself falling asleep, and catching a maid by the arm as she brought mugs of ale to an adjacent table, I bade her wake me up at dusk, should I doze off. I did.

"Master?" She gently rocked my shoulder, and coming to, the noise of the common area filling my mind, I awoke. My neck ached for I'd slept crookedly, and looking around I noticed my food had been removed, as had the pitcher of ale, though a mug half full remained.

'You slept like a baby,' said Wisp across my conscious thoughts. *'I left you alone,'* my dream companion mused.

"Why?" I spoke aloud.

"You asked me to wake you, before it got dark, master." The girl was marginally surprised by my question, not realising I hadn't spoken to her.

"Urh, oh, no, you did right. What time is it?" I asked the girl, whilst looking around.

"Oh, it must be five or six hours before midnight," and she asked if there was anything else she could do.

"Just my clothes."

"I'll see where they are." And she walked off, holding a tray full of wooden plates, mugs and the like.

'Sandy says you are invited to join Tam for dinner at dusk, if you like?' said Wisp. *'I told Sandy you'd wanted to.'*

'Wisp, it's dusk now! Why didn't you wake me up?'

'I was about to, I was exploring the city.'

Bloody hell. I followed the girl to the bar. The innkeeper, serving several customers, glanced at me.

"I need my clothes now," I said bluntly, ungraciously, and the innkeeper turned around and bellowed for 'Clegg'.

No cloak, nor mail, neither axe nor helm, I walked through Gledrill carrying a small chest. The streets were still busy, people finishing business late, the evening air not unpleasant, merchants staying open until customers left and no new arrived.

The castle – a fortification under a rocky mass that jutted out casting a shadow in daytime, the building protecting against attack on two sides, the great walls formidable, and as I approached, arriving as dusk ended and night fell, two massive wooden gates were shut, yet a small door inserted in the right leaf stood ajar, giant sconces casting flaming light either side of the gates.

A few men stood about, and a broken down cart lay leaning on its side, the axle broken and a wheel removed, although there were no goods left behind.

A soldier, noticing me, stood to attention, and formally blocked my way, asking for my name.

"Miller." And before I had scarce finished uttering, "I am expected," a servant, a courtier appeared and warmly greeted me, bidding me to follow, for I was expected and he would lead the way.

Bloody sight better than the last time I tried to access a castle, I thought, and being led through the castle grounds and into the main keep, I told Wisp he was forbidden to enter Tam's mind.

I had never seen the inside of Tam's castle, other than spending two days recuperating in a suite of rooms, locked from external trespass, whilst I recovered from injuries sustained during a combat lesson with Grimnir. Although there was one basement room that I been ported to and I had been led out, not aware of my surroundings. This was new, and I marvelled at the rich tapestries hung on walls, and the cleanliness of the place.

People watched as I followed my guide, wondering who this half-orc was, causing gossip and speculation, and whilst I was dressed in clean attire, it was clear that they thought me shabby. *Sod them.* I hoped I would never turn into a dandy.

"You'll forgive me, sir," said my guide, "but when we reach Lady Bluebottle's reception chambers, you will be asked to leave your weapons outside the entrance." And he looked at the small chest wondering whether I could conceal a weapon inside.

"No weapons inside the box, but with Lord Grimnir's presence, I doubt I'll pose much of a threat."

My guide looked nonplussed, befuddled by my words, trying to formulate a response, for I'd guessed rightly, and now he would appear obtuse should he press a request to peer within.

*

Tam and Grimnir sit in comfortable chairs in a room approximately twenty-four feet by nineteen feet, a fire burning within a small marble fireplace; beautiful oil lamps hang from wooden timber posts lining each corner, a triple leafed window has one pane slightly ajar, and small oak tables are drawn close to the fireplace. Piles of papers are scattered across a larger table near to where I enter.

Tam rose from her chair, and thanking my guide, who bowed and departed, walked warmly towards me.

"Let me see your face," she said, as I lowered my head, effectively bowing, though that was not the intent.

Reaching up touching my old scar, she kissed me. "I see you've used a healing spell, your old scar is almost gone." She squeezed my hand. "It's lovely to see you again."

"He should be covered in scars the way he picks fights all the time," laughed Grimnir, who didn't bother getting up." And as Tam scowled, "I've already seen the bugger today, that's more than enough." Adding, "Pull up a chair, young Miller, and tell us what's been happening."

I apologised for being late, a lesson learnt from Thrandar, and requesting that we avoid sitting at a large table, and yes, I'd be happy to eat where we sat, the usual pleasantries, I pulled a small stool between us and placed my chest in front of them.

"It's open, not trapped, there was a key locked inside when I found it." I waited for comment.

"What's Miller found?" said Grimnir, reaching forward and opening the chest, and with no surprise, lifting out the gems whilst passing the letter to Tam.

Grimnir rose from his chair as Tam increased the flame on a small lamp hung near the fireplace, unfolded the vellum letter and started to read.

As I watched, Grimnir scraped the gems together and walked into a corner of the room and under the glow of a brighter lamp started to appraise the stones, holding each one up to study.

"Not bad. Where did you get them?" And not waiting for a reply, "I've seen worse."

With Grimnir sat down, the gems returned to the chest, sitting in silence we watched Tam who seemed totally disinterested in the gems, intent upon the letter before eventually reaching for the chest, taking the key, examining it and placing it in the escutcheon, locking and unlocking the chest several times, pressing on the lid.

"How much, Grimnir?" She enquired as she passed him the letter.

"About twelve hundred." He reached out and took it from Tam's outstretched hand.

'Less than you hoped,' Wisp said. *'And you do know I'm stuck inside your head, I can't get out.'*

'You aren't meant to get out, I told you not to read her thoughts.'

'You know I wouldn't, you told me not to, but I'm still stuck,' and to emphasise the point, *'really stuck, there's*

some magic at play.'

Several minutes passed in silence.

"May I keep the letter?" Tam said, looking at me.

"Yes, of course, what do you think?" For having read the letter twice, I knew it was an offering from the Avarti to Edric's cause, sent to aid Hjalmar.

"We have some of the Avarti down in Hedgetown," said Grimnir, frowning.

"And here in Cragtor too." Tam spoke slowly. "Where did you find the chest?" She looked at me, and I noticed she hadn't asked *how* I found it.

"East of the Grey Mountains, ten miles from a tiny town called Stours, though I don't think they came from there," adding, "they may have come from your side."

"Sandy says you're hiring men; orcs he actually said." And as Tam said that, Grimnir pulled a face, looking down at his boots.

"Thought you'd do better than orcs, Miller. Never trust an orc," Grimnir rumbled, sternly, adding a few more choice words.

"Actually I'm hiring men and half-orcs, though I confess there are a handful of orcs, I acquired them by accident. How does Sandy know?" I looked at Grimnir. "Orcs don't drink the blood of human babies, aren't spawned from hell and don't sacrifice their own children to infernal gods of the abyss, despite what people think."

"No, just ninety percent of them do." Grimnir was not impressed, and changing the subject asked Tam, "Do we arrest them?"

"No, not yet, we need to know who is affiliated and knowing their allegiance gives us an advantage," said Tam. "And please, will you two not fall out with each other?"

Grimnir mumbled, and I, too proud to admit that Grimnir was mostly correct, let the matter drop.

"So who is the hidden sorcerer?" Tam mused, and I looked blank, not understanding the question. The fact that the key fitted the chest was an oversight; now realising the pilgrims had no means of accessing the contents it explained why I had been unable to find a key when searching their camp. It was inside the chest, unlockable only by magic. And then the penny dropped.

"Who locked the chest to begin with?" I said quietly, understanding what Tam had deduced so easily.

"Yes indeed, we need to find out… May I keep them, please?" asked Tam, meaning the chest as well as the letter.

"The chest is beautifully made, not many craftsmen have the skill. It should be easy to find out who order its construction, or bought it." Tam once more studied the craftsmanship.

After explaining everything to Grimnir, I asked how to get my gems converted into silver at the best possible exchange rate.

"What, all of it in silver?" said Grimnir. "It'll weigh a ton, but there's no doubt with trouble coming, some of the merchants are converting silver and gold, wanting portable wealth. You'll do better in Hedgetown."

"Twelve hundred silver isn't too much of a problem, I've carried half that much for some time, although a bit of it is in gold and amber." But I'd missed the point.

"No, you're wrong," said Grimnir, smiling.

"How much did you say the gems were worth?"

"You'll get about twelve hundred gold in Cragtor, thirteen if you're lucky in Hedgetown." And he looked at me, knowing it was more than I had ever owned. "Are you coming down to Hedgetown with me tomorrow?"

I sat there grinning, I couldn't help myself, and Grimnir laughed, for thirteen hundred gold was twenty-six thousand silver pieces, enough to build an army, at least east of the mountains.

The evening passed with numerous discussion about preparations for war, and that Tam and Grimnir's successfully recruitment drive was going well.

"Hard to train two hundred lads and scoundrels, it's bad enough trying to bring our current men up to a decent standard," mulled Grimnir. "As you so painfully demonstrated outside the gates today, Miller." He looked first at me then Tam, as I averted my gaze, for the men were indeed hopeless. "Miller was playing with four of them, who were desperately trying to arrest him, and you know how rubbish Miller is," he said, looking at Tam.

Ignoring Grimnir's jest, and being slightly flattered, I was eager to get my silver and head back, knowing, or rather suspecting that twenty-six thousand silver might still take a few days to gather.

"Has your great hall changed, the area around the fireplace, below the carved windows?" I asked Grimnir, and he, not too puzzled, suspected why I asked.

"Time's pressing for you, Miller? Want me to hold your hand?"

"Please, I need to be back east of the Grey Mountains within five or six days, and I've a mind to visit a fletcher if I'm in Hedgetown."

I spent the night in Tam's fortress, not attempting to gain access at the 'Haggard Hen' for it was past midnight, and I was too drunk, not least I hadn't realised just how much the gems were worth and although Cragtor was safe even after dark, I wished to avoid risk. My mother's human nature resisting my fey orcish spirit.

At first light I returned to the Hen; the door stood ajar, whilst stable hands and the innkeeper prepared for the day ahead.

"Didn't see you last night," said the innkeeper. "I can't keep the doors open all night in case you return."

Not my problem, I pay you enough. I chose not to say it out loud.

With my possessions recovered, and waiting an extra hour for the repaired cloak to arrive, I settled my bill, laying an extra silver piece in the hands of the innkeeper. "To settle the cost of the cloak, and my thanks." I headed back to the castle. And was stopped again.

Wisp had found that upon leaving the castle entrance he was no longer confined, able to wander unimpeded and as we approached the castle, it was only upon entering under the arch, through the gates, that he informed me he was once again constrained.

Tam wished me well, smiling and reminding me of the rusty nail should I ever need to return; it was a nail hidden in my pack that could transport me, only once, from any distance to her chambers deep within the castle and I learned that it could only transport myself, not my hound, a gift given by her to me months before, and I hadn't forgotten it was there.

"Neither you nor anyone else can port into this stronghold," she had said. "The nail will work, but not by your own skills, a precaution against Edric."

So Grimnir, having informed his two soldiers he was returning on a swifter steed, walked with me out of town heading for a small wood yet having to tell the curious to piss off, or at least I did, we arrived at a small copse a quarter mile from the edge of town.

"Bloody hell! Miller, I'm not looking forward to this. Are you sure you can do it?" And he did look decidedly uncomfortable. "I thought you were only good for a few hundred yards?"

"I've been practising. I can usually get it right, but I need to try." And smiling, Grimnir didn't know whether I was serious or jesting.

"Right, hold tight to my hand, I don't want to lose you halfway, no idea where you would end up." I was enjoying Grimnir's discomfort.

"Shit," Grimnir said, as hidden within the wood, I started uttering words that he'd never heard Tam use, and we were gone.

CHAPTER 7

Estridge has been in view for the best part of the day, and tacking close to the wind, the schooner makes steady progress, having to 'go about' twice before gaining the bearing needed for the final approach.

It seems to take an age, yet the courtier has found his sea legs, able to appreciate the intricacies of sailing, and for the last week he has observed and learned a lot, losing much of his surliness, and on occasion asking to take the wheel, marvelling at the strength required to hold the rudder, gaining a feel for the roll and pitch, turning the wheel slightly as the vessel plunges down before each rising wave, minimising the yaw, anticipating as a novice the subtleties of helmsmanship.

Standing now, near the bow, watching Estridge approach, keen to bathe and secure lodgings for the night, a sailor counsels against staying too long 'forward'. "We'll be jibing in a minute." He has no idea what 'jibing' is, but accepts the counsel, as walking back the mainsails are lowered and the foremost jib flaps in the wind, men scrabbling to furl and secure, as the one remaining jib stays taut.

Returning to the aft deck, he watches the last two hundred yards, the main docks approaching, passing alongside pontoons, and other vessels at anchor.

As the stern of the boat swings around the second jib flaps then tightens, snapping into position where moments before he had stood, helping swing the boat, but for a moment, as it too is loosed and gathered in. The boat swings gently under its own momentum, and the courtier acknowledges the skill. Gently the vessel inches parallel to the quay, mooring ropes thrown to dockers, stevedores waiting to unload the cargo.

Slightly tutored in patience, at least towards the master of this vessel, he now understands there are jobs to be done before he can disembark, yet he command his servants to be ready. "I'll be walking, but you need to hurry and find me suitable accommodation."

Finally walking down the gangplank, he nods to the master, a token gesture, but more than he would normally do, and stepping onto dry land, he staggers, grabbing the shoulder of a passing sailor, steadying himself.

"You'll get your land legs back in a day or two!" shouts the ship's master. "Take it steady, you'll be fine." And turning away, he hides his smile.

Servants having been sent ahead, the courtier

walks in an almost straight line to the end of the quay, salt encrusted, and not so sure he's as hungry as he thought he was an hour before.

Estridge has two roads, one heading to Hedgetown, the larger of the two, and another towards Cragtor, and he takes the most northerly arriving clean and fresh at the gates of the city the evening of the third day from disembarkation.

His golden brooch that fastens around his neck, a clasp for his cloak, is the last of his wealth for having secured lodging and passage, both for himself and his servants, and travelling farther than he thought originally to do, he is worried. There are three silver hair fasteners in his bag, but he has no intension of trading them. Badges of rank, and precious to him, he intends to sell the clasp, and replace it with a silver one of lesser worth, keeping the difference for his immediate expenses, unless of course Lady Bluebottle will secure his return passage.

Standing before the gates, a small trap carrying his baggage, he remonstrates with the guards. "I'm an ambassador to the king, and am exempt from tithes." Indeed he looks like an emissary; his cloak and clothing having been washed and with two servants modestly dressed beside him, his baggage being of fine quality, they have no reason to doubt him.

Likewise stood in front of the half-open castle gates, he looks up at the great tor, a brooding shadow in the failing light, casting a gloom over half the castle below, whilst one of Tam's servants invites him to follow, suitable accommodation being found – a small suite of rooms, appropriate for his rank; other rooms for his servants nearby.

"The Lady Bluebottle is in her study, and will be informed of your arrival," says one of Tam's aides. "I will be stationed outside your chambers, should you need me. Have you eaten, sir?"

"No, no need. I might stretch my legs, in an hour or so."

At last, in civilised company, the emissary feels comfortable. Indeed he wouldn't mind sleeping, perhaps a little later, and hopes Lady Bluebottle will see him the next day.

"Please could you inform Her Ladyship, that if it is agreeable, I'll retire in a few hours, but I would welcome the opportunity to meet with her on the morrow!" And with that he closes the door, and without his own servants' attention seeks the comfort of his own company, pouring wine from a silver and glass decanter, before wandering around his quarters examining the fabulously expensive furniture and realising civilisation doesn't stop ten miles from Culanun city boundaries.

Tam is deep in thought, meditating in the basement of her castle, journeying with Sandy, gathering her powers of craft, yet part of her consciousness dwells still in her chamber, abilities so much more advanced than Miller's or any known sorcerer within four hundred miles.

She waits, hours passing in the physical world, determined to sense all the practitioners of magic, looking for eddies within the connective energies, watching for ripples, the flow signifying the harvesting of power by others skilled in craft.

Knowing someone has knocked on her door,

despite her instructions not to be disturbed, she leaves Sandy to carry on and gradually she re-emerges, her room lit by a lamp that gives no heat or smoke, seemingly burning endlessly, and rising from her cushion, unlocking the door, and sitting upon a fine delicate chair, a desk in front of her, quills and parchment and books piled high, she commands the person to enter.

"Your pardon, my lady." Her personal valet enters through the doorway. "An emissary from the king has arrived, and whilst we've tended to his needs he seeks an audience with you, preferably tomorrow."

"What is the current hour, Pip?" asks Tam.

"Three hours before midnight, my lady,"

"Very well, I'll see him tomorrow at noon." And thinking she had so much to do, she added, "I'll need you to return here two hours after midnight, I'll need to get some sleep… Pass on my regards and apologies for not greeting him upon his arrival."

And with Pip leaving, Tam locks the door, takes a little wine – not too much – and sits once more upon her cushion lain upon the floor.

Sinking again, joining Sandy she concentrates; hours pass, and as midnight falls, she detects movement in the gentle ripples of the earth song in the snippets of power, locally, within a mile, and Sandy heads in the direction, exploring, searching as she tries to triangulate, moving her mind just below the ocean of altered perceptions. Sensing the power of the sorcerer, not great, their depth shallow, she gains a bearings on the likely epicentre, and rising back into consciousness, she knows Sandy will report shortly.

'*At last.*' For she has spent hours waiting, unproductively, for the hidden sorcerer to reveal him or herself, and now she would shortly know where.

'*I need Miller's help.*' And opening her door, she calls for a servant.

"Tell Pip I'm not to be disturbed until dawn," adding with emphasis, "regardless of circumstance, and fetch me Glamdrun, urgently. Glamdrun before Pip. Now… run."

And hearing the urgency in her voice, imagining some dread circumstance had befallen his mistress, the servant speeds away, as Sandy explores the town seeking a location, and after several minutes returns, hovering below the chamber floor, waiting to be summoned.

"Sandy." Tam spoke so gently, and the great elemental rose from the ground as a soldier rushes down the passageway, the door ajar, his feet clattering on the stone flags, his sword and armour clinking as he runs, and Tam stepping out into the corridor, preventing his entrance, standing diminutive before a six-foot-tall warrior, his studded vest not fastened tight nor his boots fully laced, having sped from his quarters, close within the castle, receiving an urgent summons.

"Your pardon, my lady, I had just finished my duty, and am inappropriately dressed."

"You are fine, Glamdrun, wait outside, but a moment." And Tam, returning to her basement chamber, closing the door, asks Sandy if he has the location.

'*A small building, west of the far market square close to the northern gate.'* Sandy speaks across her mind, a connection that is both telepathic and empathic.

'I need Miller here as soon as possible. Tell him to use the nail. Go swiftly, he may be with Grimnir in Hedgetown.' And Sandy sinks into the floor.

Opening the door once more, Tam invites Glamdrun inside, his vest almost fastened tight.

"Miller will be… is… in my private chamber suite. You will bring him here to me, but you will only enter my chamber in half an hour's time. He's there with my permission and is to be treated with proper manners." She adds, "I know you aren't endeared to him, but he is helping me on an urgent matter."

Glamdrun listens as Tam gives instructions for twenty soldiers to gather at the northern gate. "Order the soldiers first, and bring Miller to me here, personally. He mustn't be hindered."

Glamdrun fastens his boots as he listens, and springs away when Tam is finished.

"And Glamdrun," Tam says as he springs away, yet hesitating upon hearing his name, "thank you!"

*

As for me, I was preparing to depart for an oak tree with a ball of roots shaped like a bowl, the remains of a fire half covered in leaves, blackened embers as reaffirmed to me by Wisp and as I stood in front of Grimnir adjusting three large saddle bags slung over my shoulders, a quiver full of fine arrows strapped to the top of my pack, I wished him well, thanking him for all his goodwill, not least exchanging my gems for silver, albeit Grimnir had been slightly pessimistic. I had gained two hundred and twenty-seven more pieces of silver than expected.

My amber had been appraised, and was worth less than hoped, yet I had a rough valuation for the other pieces now in Flukaggrrr's possession.

Grimnir's antechamber, a private room attached to his great hall, acted as a study and sanctuary, and ready to depart, Grimnir couldn't resist the urge to give advice.

"Right then, you miserable bugger, make sure you don't hire any more orcs – they're not worth it."

"Don't you want to come over to my side of the mountains and have some proper fights?" Shaking his hand, ready to utter my spell, Wisp said Sandy was approaching, and as I thought of him I could in turn feel his arrival, my affinity to the earth heightening my awareness.

We were not on the ground floor of Grimnir's castle, and accordingly Sandy spoke through Wisp, though I could half hear the words, knowing Tam wanted me. Only upon hearing 'nail' being mentioned, did I drop my bags, the silver crashing to the floor, waiting for Wisp to accurately explain, and relaying to Grimnir the news he threw back cloth covers from a mirror, an ancient device he could use to communicate with Tam, as I rummaged in my pack seeking a hidden seam, searching for a rusty bent nail hidden within.

I waited long enough for Tam to reassure Grimnir that he wasn't needed, it was mainly for Wisp's skill of reading minds that I was being requested, 'summoned', so to speak, and time was of the essence.

Leaving everything on the floor, I held the nail in my right hand, and actioned the glimmer, porting to Tam's chamber, alone. She wasn't there, and neither was Wisp.

Tam's chambers, to be exact her bedchambers, consisted of two large and two small rooms located in a wing of the fortress, locked via one large oak and iron bound door. An internal locking mechanism secured unauthorised access. The furniture was magnificent; a large raised bed with several cupboards, tables and softly sprung chairs.

I had stayed in these quarters whilst convalescing, hidden from the rest of the castle for none were allowed access, except the maids and perhaps her valet but only with Tam's prior permission, and walking to the door, unaware of instructions given to Glamdrun I found the door locked tight, with no obvious means of opening.

Tam knew I would be ported here, unable to exit, so knocking loudly and gaining no immediate reply, I decided to sit as once before in the largest of her padded chairs and wait, looking around at the tapestries hung upon the wall, trying to sense Wisp, but gaining no hint of union, nor echo of awareness.

Glamdrun released me from the room six minutes after I arrived, yet he didn't know why I was required. Trying to remember the winding passageways, the rooms we crossed, eventually after descending stairs we arrived at Tam's basement study. Glamdrun knocked whilst I tried to remember having visited this part before, and as Tam opened the door he bowed and said he would join the men at the northern gate.

"Thank you Glamdrun… and do come in, Miller." She ushered me inside, shutting the door and explaining all that she had learned.

"I'm so sorry to delay your departure, I'll try and make amends."

"It's fine, not a problem. In any event, I'm glad to help."

"I've spent hours meditating trying to detect the gathering of graft, and whilst your presence was expected, I've found an unknown sorcerer within Cragtor."

Tam invited me to take a seat.

The seats were far too fragile for my great mass, so I piled cushions on the floor and sprawled out, adjusting my dagger as it pressed on my side.

"I need your help identifying a sorcerer that I've detected; he's currently inside a small building, possibly a house, yet I don't necessarily want to arrest him." Tam looked at me, as I smiled. "Wisp can read thoughts when people engage with you in conversation. So I was wondering if you could join the soldiers I've stationed at the north gate, and depending on what we find, I'd like you to question the occupants."

"Sure! I've no problems helping, but are you wanting an excuse? Just how blunt and deceptive do you want me to be?"

Stood outside a small house, a ground- and first-floor structure with a small yard at the rear, a pile of logs down a side path, the guards surrounded the building ready to arrest anyone who might flee. Wisp rejoined my mind, and explained we were to interrogate the people within.

Glamdrun didn't understand why I was an imperative, but it had been made clear that I, Miller, had to question the people inside, so he simply knocked on the door, apologising for the late hour, explaining, "There's been an attempted murder nearby, and we need to question you," walking in, not asking as I followed, stepping over the threshold, staring ahead in the gloom, Glamdrun's lamp hindering my night-vision, as three people backed away, their house not a hovel, simple with few luxuries.

How I wanted to assault them and with torture have them scream a confession, but I knew Tam needed to choose her timing, co-ordinating with Hedgetown what I thought would be the eradication of the Avarti.

Cogitating, knowing that when I ruled I also would equally need to show restraint, choosing times, avoiding that which delighted me – murder and mayhem – and likewise be cunning and patient as Tam demonstrated now.

The street was being woken up, part of the deception, soldiers banging on doors either side and across from the target house.

"Your names, and addresses if you don't live here," I asked, holding out a board of wood with rough parchment fastened to it, a first for a half-orc, to write, or so it would seem to those being questioned.

"Names, in case we need to question further." No crass bullying, but a firmness and purpose, indeed it was how a soldier would behave.

"Who lives here? Not all of you?"

"It's my house," said a small fellow, dressed in simple clothes, a grey waistcoat over flax shirt, tweed breeches, and soft leather shoes, and I looked around whilst Wisp read his thoughts.

Wisp could read thoughts when I associated with people or during their dreams but he was incapable of fathoming those with whom I had had no prior interaction, and as for reading thoughts, it was usually unproductive, much better accomplished during direct questioning. *Still, how to find the sorcerer?*

Three people stood in front of me and I questioned them, recording their address and where they worked, or carried out a trade. One lied about his address; he was from out of town, the cleanest and most aloof of the three. Wisp conveyed the deception, and asking to describe the street he lived in, he prevaricated, giving a location he knew a soldier might accept adjacent to the east gate.

Not the one, but a beginning. I teased, threatened as a thuggish soldier might, playing stupid and cursing my misfortunes, wishing I could cause my neighbours injury as my children were ill, hoping for an insight yet still not gaining the knowledge required.

Judging the out-of-town man likely, I asked each to step outside, questioning in turn, looking for a clue and in the end I suspected it was in fact the homeowner, not the one first suspected, yet not certain.

Finally amongst them all, I spoke a loaded statement. "If it were me I'd hang everyone on the street. None of you have any useful skills, parasites on the town, no talent amongst you."

And whilst Glamdrun held his tongue, I knew I was despised by two, and each thought of one.

Allowing Glamdrun to complete the questioning, already having the information required, I was still curious of the man from out of town. Who was he? Wisp would try and glean snippets of information when he slept.

"I think they're innocent, Glamdrun. Let's move to the next house, if you're satisfied."

CHAPTER 8

Rain drove hard across the ledge, the wind whipping around the mountainside; a late spring day, yet there was no respite in the weather.

'Check my cabin, Wisp, I'm easily within range.' And standing there cold, laden with saddle bags full of silver, I was keen to return and advance my plans to secure men.

This was my final act of craft, the energy contained within my body nearly spent, no means to cast further spells and hoping that I wouldn't find problems with the orcs at Flukaggrrr's camp. I waited five minutes, not daring to move, somewhat top heavy, the ledge only six feet wide. I didn't like heights!

'Your cabin seems as you left it, though there are only three orcs nearby. One is Berrek.'

It was what I needed to hear. Concentrating on the image contained in my head, a lamp in a corner, other equipment in a second, and thresh piled high in a third, my mattress, the camp as a whole, and uttering the words so frequently practised, I arrived early morning, cold, locked inside. Testing the door, it gave a little. Something was preventing its opening, possibly items piled against the outside, the door having no lock of its own.

An hour's further meditation and I was recharged. Three portals, three magical darts and two stun spells, one illusion, and I searched through my pack – the rusty nail recharged by Tam, and now allowing my hound Git to be ported too, along with a new healing scroll, more powerful, capable of helping three individuals at once, although only one application. And although I had forgotten I already had some blank parchment, more was secured from Tam before I left.

It was the tenth day and although I had hoped to return sooner, I was expected, so leaving my helm, backpack, bags and axe on the floor, I ported ten feet outside the door. "Berrek, where are you?" My hound sprinted towards me, barking and jumping up, excited to see me.

"Lord," came Berrek's reply, as he walked towards me. "It's good to see you safely returned."

The camp seemed deserted. "Where are the others?" I enquired.

"Chopping wood, if they haven't killed each other." And pointing around he showed me the provisions I requested, taking pride that the camp was clean and orderly, indeed my cabin had several barrels of ale piled against the door, and walking over I examined them.

"Where are the mules and cart?"

"We're using them to transport the wood. Flukaggrrr said we would need to extend the camp, so we've been making stakes and beams; the woodmen left axes and saws including rope and tackle."

"Any trouble since I've been gone? And where is Flukaggrrr?"

"He's in town, a place called Urthing, it's about twelve miles away, towards the coast," and he waved vaguely, "although we have a new member of the party, a half-orc called Tansraw. He's in Stours, trying to recruit men."

This was all excellent, but Berrek hadn't answered the first half of my question.

"And the others?"

Berrek lowered his head. "Flukaggrrr killed the goblin-killing orc, the one you bound? And another of the four caused trouble, apparently they were friends, but it's all sorted now, although another orc left after being paid," he hesitantly added. "Flukaggrrr's injured. He says it's not bad."

"How bad? Not bad enough to stop him working apparently!"

"Not good, Lord, but I think he's hoping to get his arm tended to in town." And continuing, "The perishable goods are within that cabin over there." He pointed to a log cabin nearest the palisade, yet visible from a central location.

Orcs were definitely a problem, Grimnir was right, but I wanted to create a kingdom that included men and orcs. It was going to be difficult, yet Berrek and Flukaggrrr were proof it could potentially be done.

I walked around the camp, watched the orcs cutting wood, recovered a mill stone useful for sharpening blades, and generally checked the supplies, and on occasion walked through the woods alone, lost in my thoughts, thinking how I would attack Stours, keeping most of the residents both within and without the town alive.

It would be a stepping stone, and I would try to secure competent administrators, something Berrek and Flukaggrrr, might not understand, at least Berrek.

Flukaggrrr returned two days later with an orc and three men. The men were not great, yet surprisingly the orc was compliant, both competent and willing to obey, the exact opposite of what I had expected.

"I told you no more orcs, at least not yet." And Flukaggrrr sat in front of me as I reached into my backpack, retrieving the jar of Tam's salve.

"You also gave every impression that I should use my wits, and that's what I did. He's good, isn't he? Better than Berrek? It was within the spirit of your instructions, broadly speaking."

"Yes, yes it was, but no more bloody orcs! At least not yet." And thinking that I had undermined Flukaggrrr's skill, I added, "Try not to, but yes, you did bloody well."

Flukaggrrr looked at my pot of salve, trying to roll up his sleeve but not getting past the bandage, eventually taking his filthy shirt off completely.

I peeled off the vellum cover. "Show me the injury."

Flukaggrrr revealed a bandaged arm just below the elbow, surprisingly clean and well-tended to, yet a yellow pus mixed with blood stained the cloth, and as he gently removed the drenched bandage, maggots fell to the ground.

"They tickle like mad," he said. "It's not looking great."

These maggots were added under the bandage to eat at the dead flesh, keeping the wound clean, all part of the skill and care the healer had used, a job well done, but by no means sure to succeed. Such wounds could kill if infections gained a hold.

A large piece of his forearm was sliced away from the bone, and must have hurt like shit. I ordered one of the orcs to clean the cloth bandage – it was reusable and we had nothing potentially as useful, an oversight on my part.

"This will numb the pain after a few hours and by tomorrow evening you'll be cured." I applied half of Tam's salve to the wound as an orc with filthy hands passed back the soaking bandage.

"By 'Akrraatsy and the Abyss', go and clean your fucking hands, and dry the cloth again. Wring it out or use the mangle." Furious, I stared at the half-wit. "I've seen one somewhere."

"What's a mangle, Lord?" he asked with dull eyes that betrayed his lack of intelligence.

Yet a mangle may not be known to the brightest of people, and explaining that it squeezed water from cloth, I asked Berrek to supervise.

"I've never heard of a mangle before," admitted

Flukaggrrr, as I pasted half of Tam's salve around the wound, using the flat of my knife and a finger to smooth the paste, Flukaggrrr grimacing as I unceremoniously poked his wound.

"It's used by women to squeeze water from cloth." I'd seen my mistress use one before when I was a slave; two stone rollers, one on top of the other and linen fed through the middle as a crank handle is turned, the water trickling away.

"Is this paste of yours magical?" asked Flukaggrrr, sniffing the cream and wondering if the maggots were now dispensed with.

"It acts like magic, but I don't think it is, just bloody expensive." And I looked at Flukaggrrr. "You're costing me a fortune!"

"Sorry Lord, but I'll make it up to you, just get me right and watch me slaughter a few enemies," before adding, "besides, I need to find someone my size with decent armour, remember?"

After ten minutes I reapplied the cleaned bandage, and told everyone to gather around the fire, for the weather had conveniently improved, and I wanted people to hear good news and to build camaraderie.

Sat on hewn logs, the gathered 'men' (I use the term to include everyone, but as men were the most numerous, or soon would be, the term 'men' is appropriate and generic) wanted to know the future, yet some were quarrelsome and I smashed one in the face, until totally submissive, he pled for my pardon. It succeeded in quelling insubordination.

My brutality reinforced complete authority; firmness with leadership when added with a reward proved a stimulus to complete their rapt attention. All watched remembering that I paid their wage, a quarter silver piece a day, guaranteed, a good standard in those parts.

Sitting observing them, Flukaggrrr had already told me that he had been profligate whilst securing the equipment needed, sometimes struggling to fulfil my wishes, using a little more silver that with patience might have been avoided. Two hundred and thirteen pieces remained.

"Tomorrow the salary will double. Each man, orc, and half-orc will receive a half silver piece a day." And I watched.

I cast ten silver pieces into the middle adjacent to the fire.

"This is the reward for bringing two soldiers, a little less for those less competent into my service, half if I find any not satisfactory." And I passed Flukaggrrr twenty, counting out the silver for all to see.

Tansraw received five, for he had found one half-orc, not great, but it served my purpose to show that I paid and commanded.

To say they were motivated was an understatement. Several wanted to set off immediately in the early evening, to get a head start on their peers.

We drank, yet I was not finished, and as expected men asked to see my craft, a demonstration of my power. Berrek had been talking too much.

"You're an arsehole, Berrek!" I said.

"Why? What have I done?" He looked at me innocently.

"What craft are the men enquiring of, if you haven't had verbal diarrhoea?" Yet I wasn't upset, it served my purpose to keep the men in awe.

"No one leaves until the morrow." And I rose, telling everyone to have a crap now, or clean it up before they leave.

"Are you sure you want to see?" I asked, showing a confidence that undermined theirs.

"Yes Lord," spoke Berrek, "it's not that bad," and he grinned to those around. Having witnessed small acts of craft he thought himself used to my abilities, and wanted to show off his secret knowledge in front of everyone.

So I stood up, and walked fourteen feet away and started.

I shrieked at the top of my voice, then whispered, the very act of conjuration magnified for effect, imploring nameless devils of the underworld to send me their servant. All a ruse to deceive, the words said in between the apparent invocation, convoluted words, guttural sounds, twisted vowels.

The camp, now silenced, the 'men' watching, sobering on the spot, wishing that they hadn't in jest or curiosity asked for this spectacle, sat subdued in thought, hoping I was only the modest sorcerer described by Berrek.

Under the crackle of firelight, out at the extremities of the camp, hidden beyond the fire's natural illumination, there appeared a hideous goblin wreathed in flames, hunch-backed, holding a pitchfork, standing still, until after a moment it started walking towards the fire and everyone scattered.

A pungent stench so odious filled the air, as of rotting flesh, burnt bones, a sickening smell, and as it approached me I dismissed the illusion, crying out words that seemed like a command, forbidding his approach, saying I had authority both above the heavens and below.

"No creature of the abyss holds sway over me. Begone, foulness of the deep. You have no authority here." Yet in truth simply my ability to dismiss that which I had created, an illusion. The apparition flickered and was extinguished.

The following morning, I reassured the men, allowing the terrors of the night to reinforce their obedience, cementing my position lest any thought to question me. "The devils and their minions are subject, likewise spirits of the sky." I didn't want to appear terrifying, rather simply powerful.

So it was that after two weeks I had a force of men, some bringing wives, and to keep the peace other women, those willing, were sought.

After three weeks we were selecting those we wanted, dismissing men not suitable including some hired previously, turning away more than we accepted.

Forty-one men, nineteen half-orcs, and five orcs made the camp full, despite tearing down the palisade and using the timbers to build more shelters. I alone dwelt in privacy.

The mules were in constant use, repeatedly collecting supplies, whilst those proficient with the bow hunted in the woods.

Discipline was always an issue, but with the dismissal of men and new arriving, after a while I was proud of those under Flukaggrrr's command. Order prevailed, men practised combat, testing each other, and when quarrels erupted Flukaggrrr and occasionally myself crashed heads together and thwarted chaos.

Men, orcs, and half-orcs not suitable were paid off, until such time I was nearing the fulfilment of my revised plans.

Eventually just shy of seventy stood in front of me, not including women and a few children. I had spent approximately two thousand eight hundred silver pieces in bribes, salary and such forth, not including the equipment and provisions that initially came from Flukaggrrr's fund. In all, allowing for armour, padded jerkins, arrows, daggers, swords, clubs, food and other incidentals the cost had approached a little over four thousand silver.

There had of course been spies, sent from the local towns, keen to understand the gathering threat upon their doorstep. Wisp had been kept busy, not idle for an hour. Five men during the last week were intercepted and or dismissed from the ranks, yet no man except Flukaggrrr knew my intent and I gleaned information from the captured spies, more than they thought to reveal, and they gathered little from me. All were executed, except an acolyte from the Avarti sect who I pretended admiration for – he and his god Avart.

"Lord!" He was bowing before me, desperately keen to further my conversion, and promising to teach me all the glorious wonders of his god's magnificence. "If I could teach you, and learn of your desires, perhaps with the help of my brethren we might find common accord?"

"Yes indeed, it chimes with my heart's desire!" I lied, trying to gather information from him especially with regards to Hjalmar, yet exceedingly careful not to expose the ruse.

Wisp was struggling to gain useful information on my main focus, that of Hjalmar. I needed to better understand the Avarti's association with Edric's lieutenant, of the ties that had been formed, and the politics of the area.

In the end I found out that they had small congregations throughout the eastern region, more in Urthing than Stours, until finally I felt it prudent to release him.

"Take this as a token of my goodwill." And I pressed three silver pieces into his hand. "I'll join your congregation, and learn more of you in the coming weeks."

"Lord," he couldn't stop smiling, "will you still be here, for I can bring someone more skilled in tutelage?"

"I will not disclose my plans, yet if you were not of Avart's devotion, you would be like the man I slew this morning." Indeed he had seen the latest spy summarily executed, everyone had enjoyed the entertainment.

"I will pass on your words to my elders, and may Avart's blessings rest with you."

"Hukrazz," I bellowed.

"Lord?" He came running.

"Make sure this honoured guest is not molested,

and see him safely three miles from our camp. "He is to be treated with respect, no intimidation," and waiting a second, all theatrics, "do you understand?"

"Yes Lord, I'll make sure I'll accompany him along with two other guards."

"Err, there's no need, Lord, I err, can make my own way."

"No... no you won't... I want you safe," I said. "Hukrazz, get on with it, see this devote man safely away." And my manner, the sternness of my voice brooked no further contest, indeed I needed to know which direction the man took, and three miles should, even with a change in direction give a good clue as to his final destination.

It was all bullshit, I simply wanted to learn as much as I could about the Avarti, as much for Tam and Grimnir as well as for myself.

Hukrazz reported back; he had had the wits to understand that I might want to know which direction the captured Avarti spy had taken.

"Lord?" he asked. "Are you really keen on the Avarti?"

"Why do you ask?"

"Well they're very secretive, I once had a neighbour who I think was one of their members."

"But not yourself?" And Wisp was reading his response.

'He doesn't think you're the religious kind. I can't see any semblance of charity either,' Wisp said sarcastically.

"Too many gods in this world, Hukrazz." And I

didn't give any harmful answers that might filter back to inappropriate sources, yet I learnt the spy had headed towards Urthing.

CHAPTER 9

Stood here before the gathered assembly, I gave a speech.

"You men, orcs and those of mixed blood, need a better place to call your home, a house to raise a family, decent lodgings, a reward for your skills and hard work..."

And so it went on, creating a dream of security and plenty for all, addressing wrongs done to each and every one of them, of nobles holding false lordship, of privileges denied, comfort withheld, rulership too cruel and harsh, and that I, 'The Lord', would see matters set a right.

"Tomorrow we march on Stours." And as the assembled throng contemplated the deed, knowing that many had relatives and considerable affinity to the place, I sought to allay fears of bloodshed, cruelty, and violence.

"There will be no rape or theft, no butchery, nor ruination upon the town. We shall secure that which is rightfully ours, a home to call our own. New buildings will be erected, the pompous leaders overthrown, their wealth gathered and given to each and every one, so that when we are done, each and every man, half-orc and orc in my service will stay, just so, in my service, glad to serve."

I watched, judging the mood, needing to secure not just the present but the future. "Stours is a beginning! Each of you now present will receive one hundred silver pieces." And I watched, waiting for the amount to sink in.

And to instil greater greed and obedience, "Every soldier now present will be the vanguard for the future. As towns fall in the coming months, each of you will receive the lion's share, each of you loyal and obedient to my just cause, will step forward and give his name. You will receive more than those who follow behind. Your future, your hopes and aspirations secure..."

There was a pause, and I feared I hadn't done enough, yet Flukaggrrr already primed stepped before me, shouting, "Place my name on your list, Lord," as men erupted in cheers.

Each name was taken.

One of the women could write, and given parchment, quill and ink, she sat at a bench as men filed up, the theatrics giving credence to the great scheme ahead, theirs and my fealty to each other.

I would be loyal, brutal, yes, but faithful. No Machiavellian deceit; these warriors would worship me, and I would in turn secure their future.

That night men were picketed around the camp, and a woman was caught fleeing to warn Stours, not so easily seduced by a speech – a clever woman, but her man was compromised, not wishing to lose out on the hopes of a home and a hundred silver pieces, a fortune in those parts. In the end I showed mercy, not part of my natural nature, a considered response designed to elicit the utmost loyalty, an exercise in reinforcing the righteousness of my campaign.

The woman was brought bound during the night, as I meditated. Berrek, knocking on my door and not gaining a response, knew not to enter or knock twice.

My art of craft changed, spells more suitable for the task in hand. I had in the morning paraded her before her man, and shown leniency.

Looking back, the thought of mercy makes me want to vomit, or would if the meal I ate wasn't so good, nonetheless it was prudent at the time... I lie to myself... but which part of the sentence or nuance is false? Let the reader discern.

Recalling this story, scribes sit before my feet whilst I scowl at them, sat upon a carven throne hewn from a great tree with silver threads beautifully inlaid, I am emotionally compromised. The recollection seduces my mind, remembering fealties and friendships.

The scribes look up, quills poised... recalling this proud time, so much accomplished and whilst I was so young.

In 'the early hours as the camp made ready to depart I passed my judgement upon the woman, her husband falling to a knee, begging not to be excluded, yet I didn't despise her, seeing so many women exhausted after working all day, risking their life bearing a child into the world and my greatest friend, the cleverest person I knew was female. Still, they are different, weaker, usually emotional, yet often wise, a compliment to any man fortunate enough to gain a good one.

Men cheered at the justice, a woman not given to the weightier matters of chance, or hope, and she was allowed to remain within the camp, her man more determined than ever to reward my compassion.

*

There is courage in numbers, but I wanted seven men to go ahead and secure the far side of a section of palisade. These men had to be brave, capable of acting potentially without support to precipitate an attack that should it fail would likely mean their lives were forfeit. Sitting down with ten of the local townsfolk, I took advice, learning how many guards there were, what had happened in previous situations where the town was threatened, how many of the common citizens would swell the ranks, manning the stockade alongside the militia.

Hukrazz, the orc brought into service by Flukaggrrr, suggested a night attack, with fires lit within the town as a distraction, and there certainly was merit in the lighting of fires. The militia not only acted as security, but as protection against civil unrest and any other tasks that needed rapid response; the quelling of fires would thin their numbers, and men who knew the town well suggested there were at best only twenty-eight militiamen, operating on eight-hour shifts, but that number would increase threefold if the townsmen had a chance to organise themselves.

"The men amongst us will not fight well at night," said Flukaggrrr. "It might be better if we attack at the beginning of dawn, assembling under the cover of darkness, and when fires are lit, allow half an hour for the mayhem to gather, then storm the entrance with the seven attacking from within, hopefully opening the gate as we arrive?"

"Should we not attack the Master's Hall, and make him our hostage?" asked another. "We must be fast and ruthless, killing initially so others are cowards."

In the end I gave my plan of battle, seeking a quick victory, stunning the townsfolk into submission.

Tansraw and one other would set fire to three buildings farthest from the gates as practically possible, whilst I would secure the gate with two men and as soon as twenty were inside I would lead the storming of the Great Hall, and bring the master and his family to their knees.

The rest led by Flukaggrrr would arrest those militia still in their barracks, or fight them as long as required.

"Should you be unable to swiftly subdue the guards, then as soon as the master is captured, I'll use magic to bring them all to despair."

It was agreed, or rather no one had any good counsel against my plan.

"What of the women and children here in this camp, they'll be undefended?" said a man, who was thinking of his own woman and child.

"When the town is secured, ten men will ride back to provide security. There are women here who can use the bow, and as the attack is unexpected, they'll be in little danger," I said, knowing that all needed to rest assured that their own possessions and family were without peril.

We set off the following evening, two hours after midnight, strictly speaking the morning of the day following, and that evening we ate together, a throng of men, women and children, distracted by ale and song. Yet many contemplative, dwelling in private thoughts hidden from each other, worried that their courage would not hold fast.

The blood of slaughtered animals was kept aside and mixed with earthen pigments and a little tallow, and as we left the camp, a diagonal line of blood paint was daubed across the breast of each man, myself included.

Tansraw and his companion had set off the morning before, each given one silver and two copper pieces, to secure lodgings and pay any tolls due. Packed amongst their possessions were oil skins and torches, not uncommon for travellers.

As the half-moon cast its dim shadow, we walked slowly through the woods, the orcs and half-orcs frustrated by the slow pace for they were unhindered by the faint light, yet we would have more than enough time to cover the ten to twelve miles to Stours. Indeed I worried that we might be discovered whilst waiting for the first hint of dawn.

Once again I had rearranged my spell-craft – two portal spells, an illusion and two magic darts, along with one flaming fire, the portal spells being of the highest order of my craft, and I hoped I had planned matters rightly.

And walking in single file, occasionally in pairs, we travelled in silence, not needing to tell the 'men' to keep voices subdued, for most dwelt upon the hours ahead, and it was the hardest time for nothing distracted the mind, fear being allowed free reign. Yet the promise of silver kept the numbers together, none leaving the column, slinking away, as so common when armies march in sombre mood, men losing courage and sloping off. Sixty-eight had left the camp, and sixty-eight arrived at the extremity of farmland outside of Stours' town limit.

Seventy men, and families confined to a stockade camp in the woods seemed crowded, but looking across the line of small farm holdings, houses and huts used by craftsmen, seventy seemed such a small number. Still, tiny towns such as Stours could only afford to pay for a small garrison, the taxes simply wouldn't allow for profligacy; either that or the master of this town was keeping silver back. I certainly hoped that would prove to be the case.

Two men stood next to me, my companions tasked with securing the door, and as dawn approached, an hour and a half before the sun rose, we watched.

"How are we to enter, Lord, for they won't open the gates even just for three of us?" And looking across a distance of one and a half miles, I knew we needed to start marching.

Flukaggrrr started the advance, first gathering the

men around, telling them to run silently. "The gates will be opened as we approach, but give no sound." For he knew that the alarm might be raised before he reached the stockade; farm animals, especially dogs and geese, would forewarn of trespass. Farmers might sound an alarm. Stealth would minimise the chance of failure.

As I watched the men advance closing the distance, judging the halfway mark, I turned to the two men tasked with opening the gate.

"Do you trust me?" I asked a question they could only answer positively.

"Lord, we fight beside you!" An answer of sorts, and both wondered how they could secure the gate before Flukaggrrr.

"Then both of you grasp my hand, one on either side, and close your eyes. Be courageous." And as I started uttering words, twisted sounds, one of the men tried to free his grip, yet I was stronger and didn't release him, my strength greater than his.

Arriving some sixty feet behind the gates, one of my men started screaming whilst the other looked amazed, shaken, bewildered, yet in control of his wits.

The sound of screams rent the stillness of the night, shaking the two guards awake, for they seemed almost to be dozing.

Closing the distance, they drew their swords and bade us halt.

"He has a weakness of the mind, his mother's malady. Pay no attention. It is unfortunate, perhaps he's possessed by spirits, but he's always been weak in the head."

"What's your business this hour?" And as he said that another man walked towards the two guards.

"What the bloody hell is going on?" He was pulling his belt tight, his shirt not fastened, a sword hanging loose off his belt.

"Nothing's the matter, we simply want to leave."

"No one leaves until half an 'our after sunrise, you know the rules, same in every town." And looking stern and somewhat alarmed, he asked, "But what was the screaming?" and as he said that, flames flickered above houses, the far side of town, casting at first a faint glow above the tops of rooves.

"Shit, sound the alarm." And as he said, that I loosed my magical darts, an act of craft that took only three seconds to utter.

Three darts sped from my finger, striking each man in the chest, the energy impacting, appearing to enter the body yet I knew they really only sundered soft flesh. There may or may not be wounds.

The men fell to the ground in writhing agony, as I calmly walked up to the stricken men and with my pommel clubbed each unconscious. One died for I struck too hard, but at the time I hadn't known, though I admit the impact on his skull had seemed a little strong.

"Open the bloody gate," I said to my remaining companion as he ran forward, standing now with my back to the palisade, sword held fast in my hand, watching, ready to fight, hoping I wasn't too premature.

"Cast the upright post in the ditch, but leave the main beam alone." Glancing at his progress, slow for the wood was heavy, Berrek had done it with ease, yet this man struggled.

"Shit." A townsman ran forwards, and seeing the fallen men and a brute of a half-orc with sword drawn and dressed for war waiting to slay him, turned and ran no doubt to sound the alarm.

Dropping my sword, I helped heave the vertical retaining post aloft, dropping it on the floor, and grabbing the crossbeam, my strength so much greater than most, I dragged it clear, my companion pulling each leaf of the twelve-foot doors inwards.

The gates wide open and no men upon us, I once again ordered that the upright post be dragged outside and thrown in the ditch. So much harder to re-secure the doors, and looking outside, I could see men running two hundred yards away as the grey outline of dawn appeared on the horizon an hour before sunrise.

A horn sounded out in the grey farmland, too late, and as if in answer, a horn blew much closer; the town was stirring.

"Drag it, hurry." Waiting, watching, and after two minutes the task done, I went to pick up my sword, and an arrow whistled past my shoulder. "Shit."

Edging back closer to the door, angling against the archer who seemed elusive, I beckoned my man to stand beside me.

"Steady your nerve," I said briefly, glancing down at him as I began my next act of craft. Bellowing a curse, summoning hounds from hell, all an illusion, and holding my follower flat against the roughly hewn wooden doors, my left arm pressed against his chest, I uttered sounds unearthly, shrieking in the cold morning air.

Two flaming wolf-hounds appeared, baying in the stillness and smelling of death. I sent the phantoms down the streets, not thinking of Tansraw, but certain it would cause panic to any men gathered, ready to counter attack.

If it were me, I'd be shutting the doors of my home, and trembling in a corner. Yet the creatures could cause no physical harm and after five minutes would evaporate, the spell spent, and I, having no means of directing the apparitions after they left my line of sight, no control over the direction they travelled, set them to perform concentric interconnecting loops even though that meant they passed through buildings, unimpeded by structures.

A learned person, not driven away in terror might think the behaviour artificial, and it was, but it would serve a purpose.

"You're doing well." I looked at my companion, terror written across his face, yet his courage held as the first of our men ran across a narrow bridge, through the gates, and started gathering together, Flukaggrrr the fourth to arrive.

"Bastards can run faster than me," he grinned, excusing the fact that he wasn't first through the gates.

Men gathered, ten, twenty, with more following, the bravest first, yet all keen to share in the spoils.

"Gather your men but wait one minute, there is a terror loosed within the town." And as if to confirm my point, screams echoed throughout the stillness of the dawn.

Leading my twenty men, I headed towards the Master's Hall; the beam that secured the main gate would now be used to breach security, carried by seven men.

The Master's Hall was an impressive stone and wooden structure three hundred yards away, very slightly raised, not a castle nor a fortified house, but still grand, and protected by stout oak and iron doors.

"You five men," pointing at three and pushing a further two together, "guard the rear, no one is to escape."

As the men charged the great door, the beam held as a ram. The door splintered, no doubt shuddering throughout the building, the master awoken if he wasn't already, now aware that hell was loosed upon his domain.

The second blow forced the door off one of its great hinges, and the third broke the door so that it crashed, edge first, half blocking the entrance, yet not enough to prevent my men from entering.

"Ten, stay outside, and guard, be visible." For I wanted their presence, armed warriors to dissuade any foolhardy assault. Five plus myself ran through the building thumping and slaying only one, a servant who had bravely charged the side of one of my men, mortally wounding him.

I swung my sword, as the man dressed in a vest, barefoot, tried to draw his sword free. It requires more strength than most realise to extract a blade, and the man wasn't a warrior.

He died, glancing at me as my blade and that of another of my men sliced his back, cutting through the spine. To say he twitched would normally be the case, yet his death blows were so devastating, he fell in ruins, so brutal the strokes, a crimson stain forming over his vest.

The master cowered behind his bedroom door, hoping against hope that somehow the misfortune of the morning would vanish, or that the guard would rally to his defence.

The household servants, his wife, and four children, one scarcely a baby, were gathered in the great hall, terrified, and certain their future was grim.

The master, given no chance to talk, to worm his way out of trouble, was dragged by his thinning hair and thrown to the floor alongside his family, as his wife cried hysterically, and one of his children, a young girl, thirteen perhaps, with more courage than most stared at me, stunned to silence but not afraid to make eye contact.

I terrorised one of the least courageous of his servants, a man smelling of urine, and I commanded him to reveal who was missing, and with absolutely no courage he squealed like a pig, saying there was a side door and one of his peers, a fellow servant, had probably escaped. He hadn't. I later found out he had been captured, and was entertaining the men at the rear.

Wisp returned to say that twenty-five men were resisting near the central market, but most of the militia had given up. Still, there was other sporadic resistance; the men near the market were running between buildings, shooting arrows, and Flukaggrrr, was winning, but making heavy work of it.

"Get up, you little shit." And as I hauled the master to his feet, some of his hair came away in my hand. "You are going to surrender in front of your town, and if you don't," I turned his head and shoulders to face his children, "you'll never see them alive," and I kneed him in the groin, before frog-marching him outside. Four men were commanded to guard the hall. "Kill everyone if you are assaulted." I made sure the master heard and knew. I led fifteen men away.

Flames visible as buildings burned, I sent ten of the fifteen to guard the main gate. "Take the beam with you, secure it as best you can."

With only five men, the master was pushed and kicked as we headed swiftly towards where Flukaggrrr was.

As we approached the market square four men tried to block our path, worried that they were outnumbered and ill equipped, but stubborn and brave, perhaps hoping to secure their master's release – a rescue of sorts. Yet their master, a wreck of a man, no longer dressed in finery, no longer confident, told them to lay down their arms. "The town is lost." Three did, yet one ran and I dared not use a spell to slay him, I had only limited craft left, the power within my body, somewhat reduced.

"You'd better be persuasive," I whispered in the masters ear as we entered the market square, and pushing the master forward, he knew there was no advantage in running for cover, his family held hostage, and I with a greater force capable of winning the day.

"Stop fighting, the battle is over!" I shouted as many from both sides watched this new development.

The master, shaking and fearing for his own life explained that the 'walls' were overrun, more of the 'enemy' were heading this way, that they should stop fighting.

"Say it straight, you fucking maggot."

"We have surrendered," he said and I, walking forward, risking an arrow shot, kicked the master onto his knees and shouted once more for the town to submit.

"Tell them there are more of my men ready to slaughter, you know it's true." And as he looked at Flukaggrrr's forty-plus men, and the others he had seen, and guessing there were probably others beside, and of course that his family was captured, his mind focussing on his children, he saw hopelessness.

"There are more, the town is taken." A deceit to himself... "Perhaps double what you see, are heading this way."

Bloody useless response, I thought. How could anyone hear him?

"Drop your weapons," I bellowed. "You may live in peace. I am the Lord of this town, and will slaughter any who resist, but those who comply need not fear." And I walked a little further forwards, yet not too far.

"There will be no rape nor pillage, no theft, no change in trade, but know that you owe your lives to me, you will obey me, are subject to me."

An arrow struck central in my chest, coming from a group of six that sought shelter around the edge of a building some twenty yards to my right. The arrow, failing to pass through my mail and leather jerkin still hurt; it had penetrated slightly, nonetheless a potentially lethal attempt on my life and had the arrow head been fashioned correctly then I may have been in jeopardy.

I later found out that the arrow had indeed spread the links of my mail, and stopped just the far side of my leather jerkin, its impact thwarted, barely. Had there been a little better craft in construction or strength of delivery then I would have bled. It was a concern, for despite my skill in battle and the art of craft, I was nonetheless mortal.

"If you don't surrender *now*," and I shouted the words, "you *will die*." And as two others reached for arrows from their quivers, I actioned my craft, a fire spell, twisted words uttered from strained vocal cords, and holding my hand towards the gathered archers, as two stepped slightly away from the corner of the building losing their partial concealment, a jet of flame fled from my hand, exploding in their midst. A flash of light so bright the market square was lit as though on a sunny day.

Smoke and screams filled the air, as yet another building caught fire, the corner of the thatched roof alight. Six men staggered forwards, falling to the floor, dead or ready to die.

"You there," pointing to three townsfolk, "assist those men," pointing at the stricken archers, writhing in agony, their clothes and hair aflame, "now!"

"Drop your weapons or receive the same fate." And not waiting for any chance to doubt my skills, nor giving thought to fleeing, I turned and commanded my men to secure the townsfolk's weapons. "There will be no slaughter!" I shouted, as I walked over to another group telling them to get on their knees.

"Gather everyone into the market square," I said, noticing townsfolk down side streets observing the proceeding, fearful to approach too close, smoke on the wind, fires spreading.

Ten of the militia, having been searched were divided into two groups, and with four of my strongest men supervising, were sent to tackle the flaming buildings that Tansraw had lit.

"There is a curfew in place; everyone will stay in their homes today. Anyone caught outside in the streets will be killed." I looked around as much to my own men as to the townsfolk; I wanted everyone to understand their duties and permissions.

"Any man, woman or child not behind closed doors will be slain!" I wanted to reduce the chance of further resistance. I had lost ten men dead or incapacitated during the struggle, and sixty men would be stretched, the victory not yet secure.

Runners were despatched around the town, the curfew enforced, such that more numerous patrols consisted of only two or three of my men, each walking and crossing pathways, meeting each other, and Flukaggrrr saw that it was done efficiently.

As for the lands outside of the town, the gates

were secured, and patrols headed out, informing the farmers and ancillary traders, perhaps half the population, yet with no defence, nor sufficient militia, that trade and normal activities would restart the following day.

By twelve noon, the town was mine. A few people resisting or caught running between buildings had been executed, examples to those listening behind closed doors, and Flukaggrrr had been competent; each death had been shouted in the street, the reason and consequence of disobedience. Terror kept others from venturing out.

As for the master, he tried to deny his wealth, yet when cross-examined with Wisp's assistance, reading the veracity of his statements, it was clear that he withheld a fortune the townsfolk had no knowledge of.

Of the seventy men, orcs and half-orcs that we started with we had seven dead and four injured, one of whom would probably die, but taking the four to one side, and dismissing the least injured, I sat the mortally wounded man alongside his badly injured peers, and gained their devotion.

In the Great Hall, not as great as other halls but impressive nonetheless, with the master, his family and servants watching, I opened a scroll and read words written in arcana, and used the gift Tam had given me.

Power, an incantation, energy released, pent up in the parchment, trapped when the magical spell was created, was now released as words tumbled through the air.

A dweomer formed invisible to all save myself, as a mist, lingering in the air, encompassed and enveloped the three soldiers. The mortally wounded man with a nasty tear and indent to his skull where some great club had struck was the most desperately wounded and passing in and out of consciousness.

Within three minutes, the men were kissing my boots, none so much as the man with the crushed skull, tears falling from his eyes, touching his once ruined head yet not quite understanding how he had been cured, knowing his life had been given back to him, by my hand. Gwynnru was his name.

"Gwynnru, you will take ten men on horse, and bring the women and children, all provisions that can be carried, mules, wagons and such forth. You may enter my lodging, and bring my saddle bags, do not steal, nor look inside."

As for the master? He and his family were locked within the gaol, a crude arrangement close to the barracks, but not before I had found and secured all his wealth, a sum of seventeen thousand two hundred silver pieces, made up of an assortment of silver and gold, with some fine jewellery and gems included. It was a guess, but probably accurate. I was getting better at appraising.

So much needed to be sorted; men were tired, they hadn't slept for some time and the following day might bring more fighting, for the curfew couldn't be kept in place indefinitely – people would need to move about.

By three hours after noon, Tansraw, Flukaggrrr and Hukrazz had located the local magistrate and he, fearing for his life, had been brought to the Hall along with six others, leading men within the town, and as for the master's former servants, knowing they were under the new curfew and forced to stay within the hall surrounds, they worked for me preparing food, cleaning and making provisions for the coming days ahead.

Sat on a modest chair I watched as the town officials stood trembling, fearing for their lives. These officials had presided over a small town of some three thousand souls and as they waited for me to speak they stared at the treasure lying on the floor, a chest with the lid closed yet other wealth spilt upon a rug in front of an open fire.

They, I was sure, were equally complicit in the amassing of wealth, the theft of public resources, but I imagined that what they had perceived as generous remuneration from their gaoled master paled into insignificance compared to that which the master had held back for his own benefit.

"Tomorrow, you will find accommodation for my men. Sixty-three men, some with women and children. They will receive priority, yet the single men may stay in barracks as Flukaggrrr dictates.

"You will arrange for town criers to announce that the stolen wealth amassed by your former master will be returned to each of the townspeople, every man, woman and child. Everyone will walk through the main gate, and receive payment of three silver pieces." I watched, knowing their thoughts.

"Your own crimes committed against the people will be forgiven, your own theft and corruption is excused, every accusation of mutual complicity that the master levels against you is ignored." And I hesitated. "Up to and including this moment in time."

The men stood there, understanding that matters could be so much worse.

"You have duties to perform, order to maintain and the militia needs to swear its new allegiance." I watched, judging them. "You will not be infracted upon nor your lives placed in jeopardy, yet I expect you to obey me and continue in your duty."

Wisp was reading thoughts of treachery; the most frequent thought was their desire to flee with their wealth intact before I changed my mind.

"You may keep your wealth, but you will swear your loyalty to me... now!" And I watched. "If you break your oath, leave my service, then you forfeit all rights and privilege of life both for your families and yourselves."

CHAPTER 10

On the second day Gwynnru arrived with the vast majority of the former camp's equipment, my silver contained in saddle bags, and other belongings useful for the future.

To his credit Gwynnru personally directed the delivery of my own possessions to my feet, literally dropping a few pack items, and several saddle bags, ten inches from my toes.

"It's as you requested, Lord, the women and children are safe, and I sought to only leave behind those items cheap in value, or bulky or both, if..." And he faltered.

His pre-rehearsed speech had been exemplary, but he'd forgotten his lines.

"Gwynnru, did you behave faithfully to me?"

"I did Lord! And... exactly as you requested."

"But you looked inside my bags!" I didn't know if

he had, but upon making the accusation Wisp confirmed, for Gwynnru mind had pictured his own disobedience.

"I… didn't steal anything, Lord. It's true, I… I, confess to checking I had the right bags, but I didn't take anything from you."

Wisp confirmed that Gwynnru had not stolen.

"Tomorrow you will watch where the silver goes, and after that you are confined to barracks and shovelling shit, you will then apologise once more to me, before I forgive you."

"Lord, I didn't steal anything."

"Do you think I don't know my own words? That I cannot see you lifting a corner of the saddle bag and reaching a hand inside, touching my silver, actions that I forbade?" Gwynnru was lost for words, for that was exactly how it had been, Wisp already revealing Gwynnru's own image of the deed in my head.

Three days later the master stood trembling and shitting himself, despised by every man, woman and child that marched through the main gate. A pile of nine thousand silver pieces amassed as a heap lay on the ground, a wealth he had stolen and beyond the imagination of most. The comparison to their stark poverty, their sweat and hard work lining the pockets of their corrupt master, and I wanted to win their hearts.

Each person received three whole silver pieces and was marked with ink upon their hand so they couldn't queue again; families given more, even those with babies given their due, such that a family of four received twelve.

Men were carried on stretchers, some propped up hardly able to walk, families raising their ailing relatives to one last effort of strength and as a dead man arrived, a soldier declared him disqualified.

He had died during the one-and-half-mile journey, the farthest reach of this town's projected boundaries, an authority that was meant to be patrolled and it seldom was, the guard too stretched and demoralised, weak leadership allowing for dereliction of duty, the pay too small. Either that or quartermasters withheld funds – more corruption. A mental note to myself: *Flukaggrrr would correct this,* and he did with brutality, not amongst my own men for they were initially uncorrupted, being blessed with a reward, seeking to thank me with honest duty, even the orcs, but I spent days and nights with my councillors, servants as I treated them. 'Tret the shisters', using the vernacular.

These farmers and the pioneers of the town left to fend for themselves suffered constant erosion of their lands, plagued by bandits and other scum of the earth, always, that is, until a week before taxes were collected, never seeing patrols yet always required to pay.

And now one amongst them was refused, *Another fucking injustice*, and I was wroth for the man was still warm. Reaching down and touching his chest, his skin flaking, diseased and malnourished, not by his family's lack of care, just the vagrancies and ruination of life as death prowled seeking manure for the earth.

"No!" I said loudly, wanting all those assembled to hear, and in truth I was indignant… "He paid during his life, but failed to make the last journey to these gates." And I passed his family his three silver, adding one extra piece. I fell to my knees. "I'm sorry he passed, but allow this one injustice to be undone."

It was all a deceit; I could and may yet rob them all, but as I said those words I knew the story would spread and this half-orc would be revered, or at least forgiven. So easy.

The master stood there, his wife and four children along with one retainer – an old woman not wishing to leave her mistress's side, waiting upon my judgement. The eldest daughter watched as I drew a knife and she knew my intent.

"Lord!" She fell to one knee. "If you spare him, I'll be your woman." She was fourteen or maybe fifteen, not ugly, not fat, yet neither a beauty either.

"I cannot spare your father." And I slew him in front of the town officials, my blade cutting his throat as he knelt before me, his wife sobbing uncontrollably. Her bowels opened such that shit stuck to her legs and urine as a dog terrified trickled to the floor, her children restrained by my men.

He died in shock, neither screaming nor silent, his mouth involuntarily opening and closing as he coughed rasping breaths and twitched, convulsing. He fell forward, blood pooling on the ground as the officials watched. I knew that his evidence against them died with him; he wouldn't be entirely missed yet I looked at the daughter, she who had offered herself to me.

"Your courage has bought your freedom and that of your mother, brothers and sister. You too are free to go." And I respected her for she alone of her peers had held her emotions in check, her mind so much better than theirs... And I laughed for she had still more to do.

"Am I not a townswoman also?" she asked, looking at me, yet not holding her gaze too long, controlling her shaking limbs; staring at me but for a moment so others would assume I acquiesced, gaining my leave yet none was given, gently testing, seeking boundaries for her boldness.

And reaching down without waiting for any of the assembled men to rebuke her, nor I... she took from the diminished pile eighteen silver pieces and placing them in her mother's skirt pocket, kissed her and her siblings, each individually, gaining the moment so that none might thwart her. She succeeded in her support of her mother before falling at my feet. "I shall stay with you... and obey."

A bloody good woman. I never forced myself on her, neither did I allow any man or orc to disparage her. She was to be admired in a world where intelligence or thuggery ruled; her name was Hilda.

Gwynnru watched as a wealth beyond his dreams was given away, and then was sent to shovel shit for a week.

A quarter silver piece was a good wage east of the mountains, so three silver was twelve days' wages per person, hard to earn for most people had nothing spare, living from hand to mouth. Also I decided there would be no tax for the next month, a small bonus that backfired for much trade was carried out that month and little the next, yet overall the hearts and minds of the townspeople were much improved and I managed to swell the ranks of my men to nearly a hundred soldiers, the salary a half silver a day, twice the going rate, but only for those with three months or more service. This encouraged decent warriors and I, or rather Flukaggrrr, was selective in those we chose.

During the weeks ahead, each of the men who survived and in some cases the women attached to the dead men received their one hundred silver and they all reaffirmed their oaths, glad to do so. I was faithful and loyal and they were sworn men, reliable.

It cost me about six thousand eight hundred for my men, plus eight thousand seven hundred and seventy-five silver at the gate, plus fifteen hundred for land clearance, purchase of housing, the extremities of the town growing, a total cost to myself of a little over eighteen thousand silver, allowing for a month's wage and lost taxes plus incidentals. Almost, I had broken even, for much of the master's wealth had been withheld.

My total wealth, including that brought back in saddle bags was still in excess of twenty thousand silver, yet now I had a base, a beginning, and had been terribly good, but it was never so, simply the selective application of kindness, and I had been well rewarded.

Competent officials were examined, receiving an audience with me, Wisp helping gain an insight into motivation and trust, such that after three weeks I was well established, the town attracting more farmers and traders. My soldiers, better numbered and equipped managed to secure the extremities of the land in a thorough and more competent manner than before. Peace prevailed, yet on occasion justice was demonstrably brutal and swift.

Captured brigands or officials caught in corruption were executed, their heads impaled on posts and placed outside the gates or along the edge of the road, picked and eaten by carrion. Left for weeks, their bleached skulls served as a reminder for other malefactors, never to be caught.

During the initial month, much occurred, yet one of the matters most pressing was the realisation that I was losing about fifty silver pieces per week, and whilst we might enjoy a good summer, and some months might be better than others, revenue in winter would be less.

Despite efficient and improving trade, the cost of keeping my men at ever-increasing salary was the reason the former master had maintained such a small force, along with his corruption, and I knew there was a need to expand my territory, or increase funds from other reliable sources.

As a half-orc I am massive, six foot four inches tall, a hybrid of two races, blessed with the best of each, such that to orcs I was an oversized human, a large human bastard, and to men I was the spawn of a stunted orc and a human whore who couldn't keep her legs together. It was seldom the other way around, in either respect.

The soldiers enjoyed my brash, brutal, yet fair, blunt tutelage. I would spend hours both in craft and encouraging my soldiers to fight better.

They would wager who would last the longest against me in sparring contests, using wooden weapons and leather jerkins. I enjoyed encouraging the men.

During these weeks I had enjoyed a degree of security, the men eager to impress and the townsfolk glad of the improved situation, and for the most part I was well received.

Almost without exception discipline prevailed. Flukaggrrr kept order, and Gwynnru, the man I had saved from his crushed skull, was keen to guard me; having completed his punishment he following me around whenever I wandered through town.

"My woman's expecting a baby, Lord. I want to name him after you, if I have your leave?"

"What, 'Lord'?" I asked, somewhat taken aback.

He looked at my feet and mumbled something about 'Miller'.

"Bloody hell." It was a rubbish name and I had tried to lose it, obviously with little success, and so looking at Gwynnru I asked, "What if it's a girl?"

"A girl?" He looked nonplussed.

"Bloody crap name for a girl." And I teased him, yet was flattered.

A month from the capture of Stours I received a visit, someone I knew.

Sat in front of my fire, several servants in attendance whilst rebuking Hukrazz, the amazingly competent orc that Flukaggrrr had secured against my wishes, he, listening carefully to my words grew in my esteem.

"I need to increase my soldiers to one hundred and thirty men," and scratching a flea away, cursing that someone hadn't kept my clothes clean, "Flukaggrrr knows this, so you need to enlist more archers."

"Lord, I'll need authority to select the best men to train the newcomers and I'll meet resistance."

Wisp said that Tam was requesting an audience.

"How the hell does she speak to you? Do you mean Sandy?" Hukrazz had no idea what I was saying.

'No, it's Tam. I don't know how, but I can hear her.'

"What do you mean you don't know?" I spoke aloud. "It's your bloody reality, your domain!" And gathering my wits, I added, "Do you even know what time it is?"

'No! Not unless I look through your eyes, but I guess it's not too late?'

"That's irrelevant. How does Tam speak to you?" But I'd already subconsciously signalled to Wisp that it was fine.

"Fuck off, Hukrazz."

And he, somewhat taken aback by my strange words and dismissal, left the room bowing.

"Stop bloody bowing, and yes, tell Flukaggrrr that you have priority, now piss off!

"You servants, get out of the room, all of you, *now*. Out. Bloody well *OUT*." And I stared at a man stoking the fire. "Bugger off. Get out, **NOW!**"

'I already said you probably would,' spoke Wisp.

"Of course I will."

*

"That was close," mutters the diplomat to himself as he walks back somewhat later than expected, passing homes shuttered and silent for the night, people locked within their homes or trade premises, dwellings that sufficed as both.

The roads and passageways of Cragtor are surprisingly well paved, and as for soldiers he passes along the way, they whilst studying him for the most part ignore him, his freedom unrestricted, no questioning. He feels secure, not threatened, a surprise for his first visit to the edge of the kingdom, and his hidden knife not needed.

Conflicted in obligation, having learned of the Avarti's affiliation to Edric and yet in the employ of the King, he wonders whether to pass on the message entrusted to him, scrolls he had carried from Culanun to be personally presented to Lady Bluebottle, scrolls he was sure instructed Tam and by her association also Lord Grimnir, no doubt commanding their urgent support for the defence of the realm, likely an order to send troops northwards.

This was unexpected yet being a devote follower of the god Avart, he would not fail in his religious duties and any support for the advancement of Avart's glory was of paramount importance.

I'll burn the scrolls, and find an excuse for my visit. And thinking these thoughts, being distracted during the short distance, he approaches the castle. Removing three toggles from his hair, a sign of his religious responsibilities, and allowing a simple silver band to hold his hair in place, he walked through the gates of Tam's well-guarded citadel.

Bloody hell. The news he had received from Rockula, the plans to support Edric, were a real nuisance. *I've family in jeopardy. What of my nieces and cousins, my wife's family in Halstaff and those in tiny villages dotted around the kingdom? Some simply hamlets too small to be listed on maps, insignificant to be shown by any official cartographer.*

A man perplexed, and not really taking note he follows a warden to his quarters deep in thought, wondering how much time he has to order his finances, until arriving outside his quarters his guide bids him goodnight and casting his thoughts aside he notices a different servant sat outside his door.

"I'll have three well-cooked small sausages, ham, cheese and fresh bread," and emphasising the freshness, "make sure it's baked that morning," and he hesitates, remembering his appointment at noon, "three hours before midday." *That will allow time to prepare and concoct a story,* he thinks as he enters his room without any expression of gratitude to the attendee.

The door now closed, he turns the wick up on two lamps and reaches for some wine.

Bloody hell! I'll be unemployed and I'll need to act fast when I get back. He's worried that he needs to liquidate his assets and at the outset of war, property, his modest twelve acres of land, is not likely to fetch a premium price.

Damn!

Tam spends the next one hour with Miller, fashioning a new version of the rusty nail portal and handing him a healing scroll, plus liaising with Pip and a select few of her guard, questioning them on the Avarti, using no act of craft, no spell, but relying on her intuition, judging who she can trust, for she now has names, Rockula's being the most important.

Yet tomorrow an emissary from the king will be diplomatically berating her, requesting a reason for the lack of soldiers sent in support of Culanun, and she needs to sleep, so Miller having left the castle grounds and walking out into the early hours of the morning yet accompanied to the city gates by one of her guard, enjoys no infraction, watching as the great gates unfold before his command – an orc given respect. She retires for the night, the weight of duty resting upon her shoulders, responsibilities and obligations she doesn't enjoy.

The following morning the courtier burns his scrolls upon a fire, lit an hour before he rose; indeed he half awoke hearing movement in a side room, yet not certain as the sounds of a strange dwelling are always disturbing upon his sleep.

A knock upon his chamber some three hours before midday, and the courtier awakes expecting to bathe, and is somewhat put out by the news they hadn't anticipated his need in this regard. Nonetheless, the main room of his suite is furnished well and his breakfast arrives a few minutes later. Indeed he hasn't finished burning the last of two scrolls; half charred outlines rest atop the logs almost consumed, as he pokes at the edges, making sure no evidence remains amongst the embers.

"If you want, sir, I can arrange for hot water to be boiled?" He looks up, a little startled, as he recognises this man, Thrandar, the servant he'd met briefly at Gledrill.

"No!" And rising from the fire, he mumbles about

the logs not set alight. "There's insufficient time." And walking over to his breakfast, set on silver platers, he's pleasantly surprised that all seems in order, touching the warm bread looking for fault, but it seems hard to find!

"How did you find the voyage, sir?" asks Thrandar, likewise recognising the courtier, trying to be cheerful, reaching a common courtesy between himself and the visitor.

The courtier ignores Thrandar, observing his chambers as light streams through stone mullions, the windows cast with crude glass, a rarity within the kingdom.

"Sir," says Thrandar, "I regret to advise that Lady Bluebottle has postponed her meeting with you for two days. I understand she's," and Thrandar is extremely diplomatic, "engrossed in matters of state."

The courtier stares at Thrandar. "I'm matters of state? What do you mean?"

Yet Thrandar has had his fill of the ignorant diplomat, and excuses himself, wistfully thinking he might be adversely reported upon, yet less than his usual charity and tack consume his thoughts.

"Yours servants are well tended, and she will summon you when she is ready."

Summon me! This is bloody outrageous. Yet he composes himself and stands there befuddled, uncertain.

CHAPTER 11

Tam is contemplative, extremely tired. She finishes a working breakfast, receiving counsel from her advisors – reports on the likely craftsmen skilled enough to create the beautifully ornate chest that Miller has left with her.

It'll take two days for news of her purge against the Avarti to reach Hedgetown, and Grimnir will need to co-ordinate his response.

Generally Tam is loath to cast spells that encroach upon the personal thoughts of others, acts of craft that detect lying or thoughts passing though the minds of those questioned, yet she has placed a ring on her finger which does just that. Having entered a secret room adjoining her private chambers she sits at a desk, illuminated by a stone that emits light, the chamber sealed by stone, no door present, accessible only by craft and unknown to any within the castle.

A small bottle is unstopped, oozing a mist that

allows breathing within this otherwise airtight chamber. Albeit there are three narrow slits to the outside world, enough for stale air to exude, staying within this enclosed space becomes uncomfortable after eleven hours or so.

It's a secret study that Tam crafted twenty-two years before. Certainly an architect might wonder at castle plans and discern a strange enclosure approximately twelve feet by ten feet, but as few are allowed into her private quarters and fewer still would look for strange anomalies in design, only three people in the whole world are alive and know of its existence. Her most secret of sanctuaries.

Aesir, Grimnir and Jambeedee know but none have the skill to enter, and as she slumps in a chair, she nods off, sleep catching up with her.

*

The following day Pip arranged for twenty of Tam's key servants to attend. Sitting waiting for their mistress to arrive, they wondered what was afoot, whether Pip had misdirected her instructions; indeed many had been dragged away from important matters of governance, and yet each was to be interviewed in turn, summoned privately before Tam and Thrandar.

Glamdrun, Tam's devote captain, captain of her personal guard, promoted only weeks before, previously under the command of Grimnir yet highly regarded, was the first to enter an anteroom adjoining the great hall. He did not understand what was occurring, yet was assigned to Tam's protection. Tam was certain of his loyalty yet the coming three days may prove a strain on his conscience.

Glamdrun entered and scowled for Tam was without any protection, his job, and he wondered whether being the first summoned pertained to her security.

Tam, a little rested, sat behind a diminutive desk seated upon a finely ornate chair. "Glamdrun, I need to cross examine you." And Glamdrun expressed dismay, a little shock, for he thought his service exemplary and beyond reproach.

"I've, always tried my best, my lady." And he bowed, worried for the next few sentences.

"Are you associated with the Avarti?" There was little point in being subtle. Tam needed to seek her allies, and then start the purge.

"No, my lady, but I know of them." He looked puzzled, and curious. "There are people in town who are. I can find someone if you need any information about them?"

"That's not my intent, Glamdrun." And Tam knew he wasn't lying. "I need you to fetch ten of your most loyal men, here, now!" Adding, "Do not discuss anything with them, neither my question to you, nor any speculation."

Glamdrun hesitated, waiting for any further command, before realising that 'now' meant immediately.

Tam waited until Glamdrun arrived back with ten of his finest men. It took him thirty-eight minutes or so, and seeing Thrandar and Pip stood outside Tam's annex, he entered and fell to one knee. Thrandar and Pip had followed him inside.

"My lady, I have assembled ten of my trusted soldiers, men-at-arms I consider most competent and loyal."

"Take a seat, Glamdrun." And Tam offered a chair to the bewildered captain. "The news you are about to hear is grievous, yet I need to know each man's allegiance." And Glamdrun, not used to seating himself in his lady's presence, looked uncomfortable and perplexed.

Thrandar and Pip watched, quill and scrolls placed on small desks aside their mistress, ready to take notes, uncertain of their own duties, but having a sense of the occasion... Serious matters were unfolding.

"The religious church known to serve the god Avart, are plotting to overthrow the Kingdom, meaning myself and his highness." And Glamdrun looked shocked, before becoming wrathful.

"Unfortunately I have no idea who serves Avart, not so much the humble cobbler or merchant, but within these walls." And Tam watched as she iterated the news. "Those ready to undermine our security or slip poison or a knife into me."

And Glamdrun was indignant, certainly surprised by what he heard yet now gathering his wits, understanding the need for Tam's questioning of him.

"My lady," and he exited his chair before falling at her feet, "I am your humble servant. I would never seek to thwart your rulership, nor that of the King."

"So..." Ignoring Glamdrun's comments and beckoning him to rise and re-seat himself, she continued. "You will each bring ten of your men before me, one at a time, and I will build a foundation for the acts of today, for today the Avarti will be detained, sadly arrested." And she thought for a moment, hoping to avoid brutality. "There will be some innocents caught today and tomorrow… It will be for me to question them." A moment's contemplative thought. "No thuggishness, Glamdrun. Children and those attached through associated will be dragged within the net." She expressed resigned sadness. "We are at the brink of war, not war yet!"

Out of a town, almost a small city comprising some fifteen thousand souls, some one hundred and ninety-two were detained.

It took the remainder of the first day for the two hundred and three men-at-arms to be questioned; a small hall had been secured, and despite Pip and Thrandar's discreet administration, rumours of detention were spreading around Cragtor, yet the real arrests would be completed the coming day or days.

The gates shut upon sundown would remain closed for the next thirty-six hours. Soldiers were stationed around the perimeters and even Sandy was reporting on movement within the farmland beyond.

Grimnir liaised with Tam via the ancient mirror, and said that he would co-ordinate his efforts, although he had not the skill to avoid leakage in his own lands, Hedgetown being less secure against malefactors. Neither did he have the wherewithal to discern motives as Tam had, nonetheless during the coming forty-eight hours much was achieved. Indeed, Tam's main prize, Rockula, lay prostrate at her feet, Glamdrun's sword not too far distant from his neck. Thrandar sat in a corner with parchment and quill ready to record events.

Very few knew of Tam's skill in craft, that is the casting of spells – a sorcerer. Thrandar knew, as some others suspected, but the practising of craft is a rare art, and even amongst her household most didn't believe rumours in this regard.

Certainly Tam had a skill in healing, her salves were legendary, sought after and extremely expensive. She had acquired an ancient 'recipe' fashioned from strange plants now grown in fields on the outskirts of town, which when combined with other herbs and allowed to ferment, produced a pain-numbing concoction that enhanced the body's healing process, such that what seemed magical, wasn't, yet remarkable results would ensue, even upon the most grievous of wounds.

Rockula probably had an idea that Tam was a sorcerer; there were rumours that she might be, indeed he had seen the eddies in the earth song, yet being unable to descend deeply, it had been as one observing from afar, not really understanding magnitudes nor with any certainty the reality of other practitioners' skill – certainly not the direction of their location and craft.

Yes, Tam was 'good' yet not naïve. She knew that forgiveness at the beginning of war would lead to the loss of perhaps hundreds of lives, and she needed information. She wouldn't resort to torture. This practitioner of craft would be shown no favours; he plotted against her lands as much as those of the kingdom, a kingdom she knew would fall, not yet, but assuredly she knew that Grimnir and herself would be sorely tested in the months and years ahead.

"Rockula." And about to question him yet

thinking for a moment, she bade Glamdrun to leave her room, not wanting anything Rockula might say of craft to be heard. "Most of the Avarti have been arrested and will rot in prison for the duration of the war, you know why?"

Tam sighed. She really didn't want to hurt the families of singular members; her conscience didn't enjoy the prospect of misery, yet she had duties to the people she ruled, lands where farmers and townsfolk would look to her for their protection.

She would try and spare the children, the women led by husbands, or when reversed those men too weak to resist their wives. Not all families were steadfast devotees.

Thrandar sat in the corner revelling in the privilege he enjoyed, one of the few people who knew of Tam's secret abilities and keeping his head down, not looking at Glamdrun who couldn't understand his dismissal, he waited, hoping his presence was not an oversight, that he was going to rise in Tam's trust, a discreet servant. And he was.

Pip may be Tam's valet, yet Thrandar was the one trusted to much of her administration; not a steward, for that rightly lay with Lord Grimnir when need arose, nonetheless Thrandar despite my saying it, was competent and very discreet.

"Lady Bluebottle, what have I done?" pled Rockula, rising to his knees, staring at the ruler of Cragtor.

"Made alliance with Edric? Or do you deny it?" Tam sat in a chair ready to slay the man should she or Thrandar be threatened.

"I've done no such thing." And as he was about to remonstrate his innocence Tam held aloft a small chest beautifully made of acacia wood inlaid with silver filigree, and Rockula was silenced, knowing that he was rightly judged, and denial was futile.

Tam cast a spell upon the man, combined with a ring that assisted in the detection of lies, compelling him to speak truthfully, even against his will. Yet such was the animosity or perhaps his devotion to his god, he resisted. It took time to gain names of leaders in Hedgetown, and of contacts, people he knew in Culanun city.

In the end Tam deemed that his powers were weak. He would still be executed the following morning, he along with two others named and complicit in this treachery. They would be tied to a stake and struck with arrows. A crowd would gather in the public square; people would watch and learn of the reason. Tam was saddened but there could be no leniency, she dared not spare him.

There might be another execution, but of the fourth man she needed more time to think.

*

Six weeks had passed since the Avarti were arrested, and Tam appeared in my hall, a minute after my servants had left. Left alone with bats and starlings roosting amongst the eaves of the hall that I was so proud of yet were no more than a shadowy imitation of her own great rooms, and she with her exemplary manners, bowed and asked if it was convenient.

"Tam," and I was so pleased to see her, "you once

said that I should not bow before you, and yet you now tease?"

"It's a fine room," said Tam as she walked up to me, looking tired and drawn. I was slightly shy, yet she was far more emotional than I, and bowing my head I, as always, allowed her to caress my face, touching my scar and looking in my eyes.

"I've never been here before." And holding my gaze for a moment, she walked to a window and looked out, before turning once more in my direction.

"It's always a pleasure to see you, Miller. Sandy reports you are now master of this town?" It wasn't really a question, yet her comments raised questions in my mind.

How does she do it? Transport with no knowledge! And as for Sandy, how would he know?

"You are welcome. Please take a seat." And I gestured to the lowest of chairs, pushing it closer to the fireplace, removing in haste scrolls I had piled nearby, pretending that my hall was always orderly.

"May I provide something to eat?" And as I said it I doubted the wine would be good enough.

Tam raised herself onto the cushions, he back not reaching the rear of the chair, and to anyone else she would have appeared comical, as a child sat upon their parents' furniture, yet never in my mind did I see her that way, though I would have a small chair fashioned in case she should ever revisit – something expensive.

"If it's not too much trouble, I would like to spend the night here. Does that cause problems?"

Now I knew, as Tam said that, there were complex matters to discuss and I was honoured to have her stay.

My house was fine for this flea-infested town, yet my mind sped across the options for Tam's comfort. In the end I would give her my quarters and appoint a servant, Hilda perhaps. Would it be safe? I was worried for whilst I was content to have an orc in attendance, it wouldn't be suitable for Tam, but Tam's security was paramount. Who was the cleanest?

Flukaggrrr, Hukrazz and Tansraw along with Gwynnru were summoned, Gwynnru appearing half an hour late.

Hilda was 'requested' to supervise my quarters, fashioning everything as a lady might desire, and Hilda looked at Tam, holding her gaze. Tam said nothing, her manners and respect absolute, observing without comment my attempts to… show off!? No, but aware that I was unaccustomed to receiving guests she sat quietly in thought.

Flukaggrrr walked in, as was his wont, he being my effective steward and my most important and trusted 'man', the orc that organised all others under me.

"Lord." And he stared at the halfling adjacent to the fire, casting a glance at Hilda as she left the hall.

"This lady, whose name is…" and I chose not to finish, looking at Tam, remembering to protect her privacy, aware that the enemy ought not know she was visiting, "is an honoured guest." And to reinforce the point, "She is to be protected beyond that given to me!"

"Lord, it shall be done." Hesitating, he asked,

"How long is the lady staying?"

"Just tonight." Tam nodded in agreement. "You will appoint Gwynnru outside my chambers. Is he here yet?"

"Hukrazz and Tansraw are outside the door, Gwynnru's not."

"Are they presentable...? More than you?"

And Flukaggrrr smiled. "No, Lord, but Gwynnru's usually clean; his wife makes him bathe every week. He's becoming very domesticated."

"Send them in, and Gwynnru when he arrives."

So it was that Hukrazz and Tansraw, two of my most competent orcs, half-orcs, were tasked with guarding the house tonight, responsible for any trespass, and Gwynnru, arriving last bowed the lowest, his debt to me immense, nothing too much trouble.

"You are under the command of this lady, a friend of great importance to me, and you will guard outside her chamber door tonight. You will not sleep nor infract upon her peace, as though your duty was to me!" And Gwynnru took his instructions seriously.

"Your followers seem loyal and genuinely keen to serve." Tam and I sat alone, occasionally interrupted as servants brought food, seeking authority to do as Hilda asked.

I watched Tam as she sat resting, listening to the crackle and pop of the fire, allowing otherwise silence to descend, free from duties, no cares but for a short while. It was early evening, and Tam seemed to doze.

Watching her, I was proud – proud that she could rest unperturbed in my modest hall, understanding a little of the cares and weight of responsibilities she carried. It was a compliment to me that she felt secure.

After twenty minutes neither moving nor infracting upon the silence, she roused herself. Looking at me watching her, she smiled. She always smiled.

"I've brought you a gift, and news. Also I would like to travel in the earth song with you this evening, please?"

So it was that I learnt of the Avarti's purge, of the men she was training, and news of war, how unexpectedly Edric had suffered a small initial defeat, and despite her misgivings Tam and Grimnir had sent a combined force of two hundred men northwards.

"It'll be going badly for Edric here too! For I intend to attack his lieutenant Hjalmar shortly, though I've a mind to take Urthing first." I was pleased that matters were not too grim west of the Grey Mountains.

"I've more than a hundred men, too much for the town to support, yet good loyal men-at-arms, competent and stalwart, and I need to maintain the momentum." I sipped a small amount of wine taken from a pitcher primarily for Tam's use. "Much has been accomplished these last few months."

And I spent the next hour explaining how I had used the wealth from the Avarti, the gems recovered, to secure the men, and won the goodwill of the townsfolk using the former master's stolen silver.

Tam smiled. "I know!"

"Bloody hell! How much do you know? Am I allowed to ask *how*?" I was somewhat annoyed that my activities weren't as private as I'd hoped.

"Only that a kind and noble half-orc presides in Stours." And Tam knew my thoughts. "You are free, you know! Much of what I hear is from spies and merchants. No act of craft watches you, at least not mine."

Then Tam told me why she was here. "There's been an attempt on Grimnir's life." And as if cold water drenched my head I sat there, stunned, looking with incredulity at her.

"If you're going to kill a dwarf, don't use poison!" she said, and I listened as Tam explained that a servant in Grimnir's household, one of the Avarti, had slipped hemlock into his wine. "Jambeedee came to his aid."

"What, the thieves guildmaster, assassin and cut-throat, the man who tried to have me killed?"

"Oh, Jambeedee's not a good man, I'll grant you that." And Tam smiled sadly, as if melancholic, recalling to mind happier days, now distant memories… times long gone.

For the first time, I almost saw a tear. "He, Grimnir and I, go back a long way." And she fell silent.

I watched, knowing I missed so much, recalling a sentence that Grimnir had said… "There's a statue beside the east gate, a representation of four strange characters." Grimnir's words when giving directions to me. I had thought it peculiar he didn't know the town's history. Those words now recalled to mind yet said a lifetime ago!

Thus I spoke, an extrapolation based on the scantest of facts, a wild stab in the dark. "And the fourth person by the east gate?"

Tam paused, looking me in the eye. "Aesir, a bowman," she said. "You are clever!"

I sat there marvelling that my guess was right, that I had plucked from the thinnest of air, a hidden secret.

"Grimnir hadn't seen Jambeedee in years, mostly he resided in Culanun, yet the guild is his. It was the first time they had seen each other for a long time, when Grimnir and Jambeedee cancelled the contract upon your life."

"But Grimnir had known where to find him?"

"It was a kindness to you, that they agreed to meet," said Tam, still deep in thought.

"One's dead and the other I haven't seen in years." I recalled Grimnir's words about a ship Tam and the dwarf owned. "Or something similar." I spoke aloud, remembering every utterance.

"Aesir – we've not seen or heard of him in more than twenty years," she added. "Aesir, Grimnir, Jambeedee and I, acquired the vessel a long time ago."

I sat in silence, privy to private history, gaining a glimpse into times past, of fealties and friendships, strained by duty and the passage of time.

"Jambeedee's banished from my land, yet he understands, he knows me and I him." And Tam shuffled in her chair, pushing a cushion backwards. "To be fair he didn't actually instigate the contract on your life, or know of your affiliation to me."

I was so bewildered; everything concerning Jambeedee, Grimnir's rule and that of Tam's was so much deeper than I, as a newly acquired associate might reasonably expect to know or comprehend.

"Grimnir," I asked, somewhat ashamed that this was not my first question, "he's alive and recovering?"

"Indeed. Dwarves are incredibly resilient to poison, but I wouldn't have allowed the outcome."

I didn't understand her words, and my guess would have been absurd for there was no power of craft available to heal, at least not directly, and I wanted to challenge Tam on her statement, but didn't, as other matters distracted.

"What are the consequences of the attempt on Grimnir's life, and has the would-be assassin been caught?"

"Yes." And Tam, troubled, looking at me with the care of a parent who worries for their children might have, said, "The Avarti are fleeing."

"Over here?"

"I'm sorry."

"Don't be!" I was wrathful. "They'll not find succour this side of the mountains." And I knew I was blessed to have Wisp.

CHAPTER 12

Patroal Irlaneson, Second Viscount of Skitol, servant to His Majesty the King of Culanun, watches from the edge of the southern market square, not quite believing his eyes.

He has an appointment with Lady Bluebottle later that afternoon, yet doubt gnaws his heart and before his eyes he witnesses the local highest priest of the Avarti strapped to a stake alongside two others. He'd heard rumours of arrests, violence against his brethren, the local assembly hall being boarded up, and seeking to validate the stories he has set off with three toggles in his hair, now removed, and he looks on in shock.

Rockula is trembling, gagged and bound, secured to a wooden stake set deep in a stone hollow erected within one of the three market squares and a large assembled crowd looks on.

The courier is jostled whilst wanting a better view

– maybe he can intercede – and as men, women and children step in front of him he finds his view diminished, no longer seeing clearly, but he hears Rockula and two other men crying for clemency, pledging obedience, denying treachery, desperate for their lives.

"May Avart give me strength. You'll be next. Flee, save yourselves from the blasphemy of the halfling bitch," says the captured sorcerer. Many other sworn words Rockula spoke; oaths of faithfulness, including expletives, curses against malefactors who dare assault or infract upon the most high god of the world, Avart.

Jeering, the crowd shout, "Traitor!" and, "Death to the wicked followers of Avart!" and then the throng grows silent as guttural sounds are screamed by Rockula.

A shout! A collective gasp as the crowd's roar changes once more in pitch and intensity, a cry from a voice he doesn't recognise. The courtier trying to regain his view commands people to step aside, and whilst one or two turning their heads do indeed shuffle sideways, still others ignore him.

A cry! The crowd shout again, rising to a crescendo and then falling away, cheers replaced by a murmur, people no longer looking forward, turning to one another, normal talk replacing shouts.

And as people gradually return to their mundane lives a few like the courtier stand watching.

Soldiers walk away leaving three dead prisoners strapped to a stake, bodies hanging limp, two or three arrows in each, and watching, Patroal Irlaneson is disgusted to see a man 'hacking' at the heads of the three corpses. A butcher's knife with serrated edge cuts and saws at the flesh and bone, decapitating the bodies as others extract arrows and tidy the square.

"Move aside," commands a soldier, and Patroal Irlaneson, Second Viscount of Skitol, doesn't protest; his courage and confidence in tatters, his arrogance dealt a devastating blow.

Walking back numbed, unable to comprehend his change in circumstance, conflicted in thought and not grasping the options still available, he, in a daze enters the castle, ignorant that he still has respect for men bow and greet him as he enters; surrounded and still receiving the trappings of authority yet his mind cannot comprehend.

Thoughts racing ahead, he wonders how he can return to Culanun and order his estate and finances. His family need to be protected and he has little silver for the voyage.

I'll be damned if I'm travelling back in the bilge of some meat-rendering coastal barge.

How fleeting his sense of well-being, how fragile and transient his security.

I'll leave the servants behind. And remembering he wants some precious possessions from his baggage, sentimental items, he starts to wallow in darkness, realising the world is changing too fast. "Sodding hell!"

Heart racing, he considers two options: either meet with Bluebottle or flee. *And if I flee I'll need to take these.* He doesn't use the word 'steal'. *These two goblets.* For upon reaching his private chambers he stands immobilised staring at a small table, the wine having been refreshed.

I don't know how to trade these items. Cut-throats, the local peasants, pond life would know. And he cringes as he thinks of the word 'pawn'... *These vessels,* looking at two beautifully expensive goblets resting upon a silver tray aside a glass and silver decanter, *it's an option,* he thinks.

*

"Now I have something for you," said Tam, reaching into a tiny purse strapped to her waist, beautifully embroidered, and as she felt within, I watched, pensive. A gift from Tam was always of interest for she didn't give away trinkets nor miscellaneous trivialities, yet I had never thought to reciprocate, a fleeting thought soon forgotten. *What would I give to be the greatest sorcerer in the world, one who is fabulously rich?* I didn't dwell upon my lack of reciprocation.

"Ah, let me see," she said to herself as her hands, small I'll admit they were, seemed to descend too deeply within her purse. She brought forth numerous objects – gems, gold, little pouches, items wrapped in cloth, and finding what she sought, she lifted out a brooch, or so it seemed, all from a space too tiny, a purse hung upon her belt.

I was wroth hearing about Grimnir and also worried that time, or the lack of it, was now potentially my enemy. Brooding for a moment, lost in my thoughts... a burning desire rose in my heart... Sod the risks, I was becoming fey, reckless. *I would march on Hjalmar, the day after tomorrow, archers be damned.*

It was as though time fell through an hourglass, and

I was watching the sands dwindle. Now given news of Grimnir's poisoning and becoming reconciled in my thoughts, I became instantly impatient.

I cared for Tam. Yes, to other orcs it's anathema, *But I've done more than most orcs ever will.* And the evening was getting darker as the sun sank below the horizon. Tam replaced her possessions, save a brooch-shaped object, and I sought Wisp, 'commanding' him to try and contact Flukaggrrr.

'I cannot, and you know I cannot.' And Wisp, knowing the hidden desires of my heart... *Just shout and bellow out the door. You normally do!'*

'Can't you send a subtle message? An intuition calling him to the hall?'

'I couldn't scare the bear from within the cave and neither can I pass on a message, it's not within my ability,' thus spoke Wisp. Perhaps I was emotional. I was.

'Bloody useless! You sent a message to me when the assassin stalked my life, why can't you do it now?' I asked.

'That was not easy, and besides, I'd been living within your head for days, yet still you almost ignored the premonition. I simply cannot do what you ask, sorry!'

"One moment, Tam." And I arose from my chair, sticking my head out the door and finding two guards, men appointed by Flukaggrrr or another under his command.

"One of you find Flukaggrrr, or Tansraw," I said, and the man nearest looked first at me then his colleague.

"Why the look!" I asked.

"Flukaggrrr and Tansraw are... off duty, Lord,

they're err… not easy to find."

"You mean they're whoring?"

"I think they're trying to sort some trouble out with one of the men, it involves two women and a husband." He hesitated. "I don't know all the facts, but someone was stabbed, and… err, not sure really."

Where the hell are they, Wisp?' And he sped from my mind, seeking…

"Knock on the door in five minutes," I said, scowling at the man whose name I didn't know. He looked blank as I gave instructions; it was clear from his facial expressions that he needed straightforward commands, not being able to extrapolate a simple point.

"See me in five minutes and I'll know where they are." And turning, I re-entered my hall.

"If I take Urthing first it will forewarn Hjalmar and from the news you brought it seems clear that I need to advance my plans."

Tam waited patiently until I had finished explaining how my spies had primarily been tasked with scouting the coastal region of Urthing and how I was trying to increase the number of archers and general men-at-arms, for Urthing would be better defended than Stours.

She listened whilst I described the way I had managed the men, paying for Flukaggrrr's freedom and the small camp he came with, when Wisp entered my head and said Flukaggrrr and Tansraw were sitting in an inn, the 'Farrier'.

"Shall we wait until your lieutenant arrives?" she

asked, as she held a small periapt in her hand – a brooch.

"No, please, I've interrupted you too much." And I had. Her time was precious and we still needed to journey in the earth song.

"This," said Tam, passing me a small golden object, "is a periapt, a charm of sorts, to be worn either around the neck or as near to your body as possible." And I reached across as she offered the item.

It was small, about an inch square, made of plain gold shaped like a small shield, yet I could see a dweomer shimmering.

"It guards against poisoning, and will activate automatically to protect your body, neutralising the poison within. I don't want Grimnir's fate to befall my favourite half-orc."

Studying it, turning it in my fingers I wondered how old it was, and holding it clenched tight within my fist, I thanked Tam for her kindness.

"It will turn to silver when discharged, yet it is permanent; the magic stored within will return after five days and the protection will exist once again."

"How old is it? Where did it come from?" And I wondered for items imbued with permanent magic were scarce, incredibly rare.

"I made it! And tonight I hope, as we descend together you will learn how, but it will exhaust us both." And Tam explained how through craft and patience magical items could be made permanent yet at great physical cost to the sorcerer.

"Oh, bloody marvellous," I said as two orcs

staggered into my hall. "You've scarcely been gone two hours, I thought you were sorting out trouble concerning a knife and a husband?"

"That was yesterday." Flukaggrrr screwed up his face. "I think," and trying not to bump into Tansraw, "I sort out too many matters to trouble you on every occasion, Lord, you'd be bored silly, and it's my job you know." He was trying hard not to slur his words.

"You're pissed."

"Can't I get pissed in peace, Lord? I've got scant time alone as it is!" He tried not to knock Tansraw over, whose eyes seemed equally unfocussed.

"Tomorrow morning I want the two of you here because we need to discuss the taking of Urthing, and I need to know the thoughts and courage of our men." It wasn't Urthing, but Isthmi, but drunken talk might misdirect and aid my plan.

Other matters were also addressed and Flukaggrrr and Tansraw stood or rather wobbled in front of me.

Flukaggrrr watched Tam, wondering whether she could be trusted, yet was beginning to have some understanding of how highly I regarded her, not privy to my past history or her name, and despite being drunk was concerned that I revealed too much in front of the halfling. He'd never seen one before, but guessed that this must be one of the rare breeds that stories tell of.

"Better make it twelve noon, Miller," said Tam.

And hearing of the name 'Miller', Flukaggrrr, grinning, looked at me.

"Go! Get out!" Yet I added, "Twelve noon, and be

sober." I would have sworn at them but Tam was with me and I held my tongue.

*

Waiting for everyone to leave and now in silence, there were only the muffled sounds from outside, along with an occasional crackle from the fire.

"When we finish our descent both you and I will be tired, yet there will be more work to be done before the evening is spent. I may need assistance in reaching my bed, likewise you will also be weak."

"I will carry you," I said.

"If you can." Tam smiled and I thought she jested until holding her gaze, watching her, I realised she wasn't.

"You know the craft of protecting yourself from arrows, your skills proficient after Wisp joined with you, but to place the application inside an object similar to the periapt is a skill you haven't acquired, nor to maintain the dweomer within such that it doesn't dissipate. This is what I hope we will achieve, or rather you will achieve this evening."

And I watched and listened, glad of the opportunity to travel once more in the earth song alongside her and Sandy.

"Similar to the periapt, an item, typically a ring can be made such that when worn you gain the ward. The ring can also be given to others to wear, but the emotional and physical weariness of creating items that are permanent has such a debilitating effect upon your body that you will hate the very thought of ever casting another act of craft." And Tam grimaced at the thought of what she and I were about to do. "You will feel unwell, physically sick for several hours... yet that feeling passes." I wondered why she would do this for me.

"I have brought a small phial, we will drink it afterwards. It will help for an hour or so, until we can rest."

And listening I wondered, how bad could it be? Did Tam exaggerate?

"There is a reason that so few permanent magical items exist. We will be descending incredibly deep, far below the realms of spirits, to an area that you may not be able to reach, but I will assist." And pausing, she looked at me, my face and hers lit by lamps held in sconces. "Do you wish to learn how to do this?"

"I do." Breaking the train of logical thoughts, I added, "Why do you do this for me?"

Tam stared at me. "You are my friend, Miller, is that not enough?"

"But why did you 'adopt me', so to speak, so many years ago? Invest in me, introduce me to Grimnir, visit me those many nights whilst I sat infested with fleas and ticks?"

Tam smiled, carefully considering her words.

"You were not wholly ruined." And she thought. "There is," slowing her words, looking at the floor, choosing with caution that which she spoke, "a consideration of others that is almost unique amongst your kind."

"But you didn't know that, even if I accept you are correct, and I'm not sure."

"Don't be, but I had an obligation to myself." And she raised her eyes to meet mine. "I'm glad of our friendship."

"As am I, but obligation? Please speak plainly."

Tam held her gaze, her eyes penetrating across the distance. "I behaved very badly to someone like you once before, and I was trying to undo the mistake... but please, Miller, you have been a blessing, an inspiration to all that condemn your bloodline, and I don't mean you're soft or weak, quite the opposite, you have a formidable strength both within the mind and body including intellect but especially of the heart.

"I don't regret my friendship, I'm glad it happened." And she thought for a while longer. "I failed in friendship once before, and wasn't a support when I should have been. You, however, are worth every second of my time. By the Grey Gods I'm glad I called on you six and a half years ago. Yes, at the start I was salving my conscience but I'll tell you straight... It was the best thing I did! I'm glad of it.

"How else is friendship started but with a chance encounter, a risk taken... and I've been well rewarded."

We both sat in silence, disturbed only by a chirp from a nest high in the rafters. The ever-present birds that sought shelter and suitable nesting platforms, it was always the way with buildings.

With instructions that no one under any circumstance should enter the hall, and with the door barred internally, Tam and I sat on the floor, a small cushion for Tam. She and I reached down, placing our palms on the cold stone flag floor.

Wisp, Tam and I descended, swiftly passing across the ocean of altered perceptions, and falling in the earth song, the beautiful music cascading all around, the sounds beautiful, colours mixing with smell and taste, all senses combined, and I relaxed, in the company of two others, three as I felt the arrival of Sandy, and down we descended. Yet I enquired of Tam, did I just need to gather parts of the song that formed my array, the snippets and connective energies to fashion my protection spell, or was there more, now or later? I watched, floating weightless, yet I was actually still descending, and I was content to await my instructor, not repeating a question, content and relaxed, without a care in the world, allowing others to share the burden of protection. I was in this regard selfish.

So for the following hour we travelled within the earth song, Sandy and Wisp roaming ahead as Tam and I gathered the strands of energy needed to create the array of complex formulae needed, that upon wakening could be actioned to create the dweomer, a protection against missiles, arrows, bolts, quarrels and darts.

Yet Tam sought other strands, faint shards almost transparent and ethereal within the earth music, faintly seen or understood, perceived in my imagination. Watching, I marvelled at how she seemed to absorb faint traces of power that were less obvious to me, until after a time unbeknownst to me, she indicated that we would need to descend deeper.

Now whilst I have an affinity to the earth and its song I am hampered by the presence of water. It is a peculiarity, unseen by others gifted in craft.

So few can hear the majesty of the song sung deep within the bowels of the ground, yet never before had any like myself been encumbered by water, as I was.

It had taken Tam and Sandy a day's experimentation to understand my disability, a handicap in one regard and a danger in the other, for far from water, a desert if you like, I am drawn too deep, indeed unable to arrest my fall; in peril, unable to ascend... dragged so deep that were it not for my ally in craft, Wisp, I would be stranded, driven mad by spirits angry at my trespass and my body would have rotted away or starved to death whilst my spirit was absent.

Before Wisp had joined with me, I was in mortal danger, yet now that risk had been removed. Nonetheless, the ability to descend is still impaired the closer to the sea and lakes I am located.

There is natural resistance of course, a sorcerer's ability to descend is finite, resisted, impeded by limitations of the mind. There are always limits; the greater the mind the greater the depth achievable.

So Tam and I descended, passing quickly though the realm of spirits, the purple haze.

Wisp, my dream companion, reinforced my mental acuity as we sped through the realm of the elementals, having sought the greatest synergies that dwelt deep within the bowels of the earth...

Not held back by the enquiring minds that asked as to my purpose, the spirit creatures that inhabit the deep places, we entered beyond, a place that was wholly new to my perception and experience, and from my perspective we headed so deep that I was unable to fall further. Willing my mind unto greater concentration, augmented by Wisp, it was to no avail, and I signalled that I was spent, exhausted in mental concentration.

"It will suffice," said Tam, and Sandy enveloped me as I perceived a mental barrier at the extremities of my understanding, not far away, but impossible for me to reach, and as we tarried in this the gloomiest of places, far below the spirit entities, and almost in silence, our thoughts muffled, the song now but a recollection far above, we were surrounded by a thickness of the earth's power, like swimming or floating through treacle. I for my part reconciled, consigned to my fate. I was in mortal danger, knowing that if Sandy released me, I would ascend a little, but ultimately there was a chance I might be unable to rise to consciousness; even with Wisp enhancing my thoughts I was in jeopardy.

"This," said Tam, "is an area before the barrier. 'Minimum Genitive', a wall between reality and imagination, a barrier between our world and planes attached to ours, but impenetrable, not quite, but in practical terms it is inviolable.

"Planes intersect near to where we are and only invitees can access the barrier, a place of unique understanding, consciousness so peculiar that the very thoughts of the gods coalesce here.

"To travel farther in thought is not within my comfort or your ability." And Sandy and Wisp were silent, neither enjoying their position for like me they were far beyond their place of comfort.

"Here we are adjacent to the founding ripples of

the world, the origin of life, yet not quite, just as close as any with sanity can venture.

"We must be swift, for time truly stands still."

"Release your strands of connective energies, Miller." And as she spoke, I could see with clarity that which before had seemed ethereal, and as she cast her power into the treacle, I watched as her snippets of connective energies were plain to behold, the strands of connective force becoming substantial, and as for me, as I released my strands they seemed as chunks of rocks cast adrift.

"Allow these snippets of power to coalesce, and count to twenty, then gather them back again. It will feel strange, like burdening your mind with memories too complex, but you must try. Gather slowly, all must be recovered."

My mind struggled to grip the task in hand, as though I was drunk, unable to concentrate, yet through sheer mental will, the last of my extended concentration, I managed to re-gather, feeling sick, not enjoying the experience.

Supported by Sandy and following Tam, we rose, passing once more into the purple haze, rising through the realm of spirit entities, assisted at first, until through natural resistance I hovered in the realm of the tiny spirits. I could sense the relief from Wisp and Sandy; more so from Sandy for Wisp was still nervous of the greater minds, and stayed close to Sandy during the ascent.

Nonetheless, I chose to complete my return to consciousness buoyed by Sandy, as washed ashore into my modest hall and waking, I felt dreadful, and seeking the bucket brought into the hall before our descent, I thought myself likely to be sick.

Tam ascended a moment after me, and taking longer to open her eyes, perhaps through experience, she reached into a pouch and removed a small phial containing a clear liquid. I had not the inclination to read what was scribbled on the small flask as we sat there, our minds filled with a power that wasn't comfortable, I for my part holding back nausea.

'You don't feel very well,' uttered Wisp, and I was not in the mood to respond. It was taking a great deal of effort to wait without moving or throwing up.

A wooden pail with iron rim and hessian strap lay in front of me and I placed my backside in the air, as my head hovered over the sides of the rim.

Twenty minutes later, breathing deeply, gradually I managed to gain a semblance of control. Still incredibly delicate, but now able to speak, gently I extricated my head from the insides of the pale, not having retched.

"We are halfway through," said Tam, and she forced a weak smile as she watched the dismay upon my face.

"Pass me your sword, please," she said, and I complied, gingerly extracting the blade from my scabbard. I'd had a scabbard made some weeks before; previously the sword had hung from metal hoops secured to my belt.

"I'll go first." And she cast her craft, without words, spending twenty minutes deep in concentration. A dweomer started to cover my sword, shimmering, yet not diluting, and after a time I worried for her, for Tam shook, quivering and shaking, swaying on the floor, until ultimately her eyes broke the concentration, and she reached for the phial and drank half the flask.

"A moment please." And she seemed ill, her face looking grey and clammy, beads of perspiration forming across her brow. She looked dreadful. "You must now cast your glimmer into the spare ring I gave you."

I noticed Tam had used the silent spell, and whilst I was less proficient in the casting of craft without words, Wisp reassured me that he was there to support, and as Tam had looked so dreadful, and I was unsure that with words I could complete the task, I began the concentration reinforced by Wisp who was less flippant than normal, caring for me, joined in the task, steadying my mind, aware that I was so desperately at the edge of my abilities, needing his aid. He with stalwart strength and determination steadied my mind, taking onboard some of my nausea, helping me to ignore the physical burdens as waves of sickness swept across my body, focusing my concentration, helping me ignore or rather blocking the signals to my brain.

Exhausted and Wisp complaining that he too was spent, I reached across to the small phial that Tam had placed in front of me, and drank the last of the 'potion', no idea what was contained within but aware that Tam would never proffer something inimical to my well-being, and after a minute, the nausea abated, but I shook, my body rebelling, my mind numbed.

I called for a guard to enter, but he was unable, for I'd locked the door internally, and Tam muttered a spell as the bolt was thrown back. I knew the words she uttered, so long ago used by myself to release padlocks binding me to chains during my slavery, and I wondered how she managed to action a spell for the very thought of doing so was abhorrent.

Nervously a head appeared around the door, aware they were commanded not to disturb, and Gwynnru was summoned who carried Tam to my bed chamber, whilst I slept outside in the corridor, Gwynnru standing watch over both of us and determined to allow no one to approach, glad of his responsibilities.

Tansraw, although pissed slept alongside me, cushions as pillows, and a blanket shared between us. The corridor was blocked at either end by guards that Tansraw agreed were under Gwynnru's orders, for he was too inebriated and glad to pass over the responsibilities to others. We slept.

So it was in this ad-hoc manner, Tam and I were guarded during that dreadful night. Wisp did not venture far, and Sandy on the ground floor, corporeal, liaised throughout the night with him, standing on guard at the foot of the stairs.

I was wroth with Tansraw.

CHAPTER 13

Patroal Irlaneson, Second Viscount of Skitol, has lost his courage, honour and integrity and summoning one of his servants, he commands that his luggage be brought immediately to his chambers. Deceiving his servants, he intends to extricate a few choice items from his luggage, items too precious to leave behind.

"We'll be departing within the next twenty-four hours after I've parleyed with Lady Bluebottle." Yet he has no intension of tarrying, indeed he is trying to calculate how to smuggle out a silver platter, the goblets, his first thought, being too bulky and probably too hard to pawn. Yet silver is silver, and the tray on which the decanter and drinking vessels rest is easier to disguise and less likely to attract attention to any would-be accomplice in crime. *After all, pawning something nondescript should be easy,* he thinks.

Not given to theft, nor illicit activities, his heart races as he places the platter under his cloak, and shaking very imperceptibly he leaves the castle, nervously acknowledging greeting from guards and fellow courtiers as he explains that he needs to stretch his legs.

There is some relief as he exits through the main castle gates, aware that in a few hours' time he is meant to meet with Lady Bluebottle, and heading for a less salubrious side of town, an area not too far from where the Avarti had held their meetings, he wallows in misery, not really knowing how he ought to proceed.

The town is busy, people pausing at merchant shops collecting provisions, traders crying out their wares, others loitering, waiting, ponies hauling carts, bales piled high on the backs of wagons, some small provisions being pushed in wheelbarrows, and people watching him, for whilst not too out of place his appearance becomes more so as he nervously walks down a narrow ginnel, a passageway at the rear of homes and premises. Stepping along cobbled alleyways, rutted and in need of repair, smoke and strange smells hang in the still air. He's increasingly nervous; even children shout after him, no doubt referring to his fine clothes, not expecting one of the gentry to walk down their neighbourhood.

"Give us a copper, mister!" And he looks at three urchins, not wanting to hesitate, but as he carries on he thinks better of it, and returns to the eldest lad, perhaps nine years old.

"Do you know anyone who buys things, er, found in the street?" He hasn't a clue how to address the question, nor even if it's safe to ask the boy. But the child knows instantly.

"You nicked something?" asks the lad.

"Found something, yes, not nicked!"

"Ma!" shouts the lad, before telling his younger siblings to stay put. "Ma will know the right person," as he heads indoors. "Ma!"

She is perhaps twenty-five years old, but age is hard to tell, and dressed in drab clothing, a stained apron hanging from her neck and fastened at her waist, her hair tied into a bob, she looks through the doorway, suspicion written across her face. Stepping out, she looks up and down the alleyway, and studying the courtier carefully, judging whether he was a threat, trap, or other unknown risk, asks, "What's your business, sir?"

"I need some coin urgently, and have something you might be interested in? But it'll cost twenty sliver pieces." And for once the courier uses his intelligence by not showing the plate hidden within his cloak.

"What is it? You'd better come inside. It's private in here."

"I'll stand in the doorway," he says, thinking it a safer option, totally unfamiliar with the intricacies of trade and haggling, and hiding the plate from plain view, he discreetly shows the large solid silver dish to the woman.

The dish is probably worth fifty silver, and is easy to cut up into shards, silver being weighed, and the woman knows she needs to summon her husband.

Neither she nor her husband have that sort of wealth, but her husband would know who did.

"Come in, sir. I'll fetch my man; he'll decide."

Patroal Irlaneson decides that the flat stool proffered seems reasonably clean, and resists the urge to wipe across the top surface with the edge of his cloak.

Sitting down, he looks around at the piles of merchandise stocked within corners and down an internal passageway.

A small stove is lit, the smoke gently rising up a tiny chimney, a copper flue successfully gathering any fumes that might otherwise drift into the room. Three irons hang upon hooks alongside pots and pans, tongs, and adjacent a small pile of wood next to the fire, yet within the greater hearth surround.

A wash tub lies half full of dirty water, positioned against a stone trough raised on wooden legs, more clothes piled underneath, buckets and barrels wedged next to the half-closed outer door.

"Sorry about the mess," she says as she pulls upon a rope that adjusts a clothes horse, a wooden rack that hangs from the ceiling.

"Go fetch your father." She pushes the elder child towards the passageway, and looking at the courtier, asks, "Would you like sum ale? It's good stuff. Bert gets pissed every night."

"No." And thinking he can't wait to get out of this hovel, he adds, "Thank you."

*

"Eighteen silver pieces!" He walks quickly towards the west gate. "I've been as good as robbed." But in truth he did well not to be, for the thought had crossed Bert's mind, yet Bert had looked at the courtier and decided he was probably too powerful and influential to risk assaulting.

A swift carriage ferries Patroal Irlaneson, Second Viscount of Skitol, to Estridge, some three hours before a search was ordered, for Tam had initially worried for his safety.

It didn't take long before she learned of his flight. Guards reported seeing him leave for Estridge just before the gates closed for the night and Tam chose not to pursue, even upon learning of his thievery.

*

I awoke lying in a pool of vomit, for Tansraw had thrown up all over me during the night, though he had staggered away before I could catch him, like a dog slinking off, tail between its legs, head lowered in disgrace.

"Bloody bastard!" As I looked at my clothing and flicked bits of half-digested food away, I smelt my arm and tunic and rose to my feet, feeling shaky, and with a slight headache.

"'Tis three hours after sunrise, Lord," spoke Gwynnru, who was grinning and trying not to laugh at my filthy state. "You might need to wash, Lord, for you smell foul."

"Really? I hadn't noticed... you ignorant turd!" I looked at the door, adding, "Is she still asleep?"

"No one's been in or out all night." Gwynnru couldn't stop grinning.

I felt dreadful; not as bad as Tansraw, or for that matter how Flukaggrrr would feel. *So much for guarding me properly.* "Bollocks, Gwynnru, it's not that funny!"

But Gwynnru clearly didn't agree, and kept sniggering as I walked down to the kitchens, looking for a servant and somewhere to douse my head, a bucket of water. I stank of beer, cheese and mutton.

Two hours later I was clean and sitting in a chair, staring at a small pewter plate with my breakfast of ham, mushrooms, bread and fried eggs. I poked at the food, nibbling upon a crust of bread, barely touching anything. I just wanted to sleep, and Tam walked into the hall accompanied by Gwynnru.

"Good morning, Miller. How do you feel?" And walking towards me, she turned her head and thanked Gwynnru for his care. "I'm surprised you were sick, for the potion should have helped prevent the nausea." Rushing from the hall, Gwynnru started laughing, as the sound became muted, the door closing behind him.

"It wasn't me, it was someone else," I mumbled as I arose slightly from my chair. "Now I know why no one makes permanent magical items."

Looking at my sword and ring, both showed the gentle signs of a dweomer cast upon them, yet the sword seemed to shimmer with a different hew, so faint. "What did you do to my sword?" I asked as she watched.

"Hold it and think of someone you know." And as I raised the sword in my hand I felt it tug to one side, pointing westwards.

"It will provide the direction of anyone you've met at least once, but not the distance, not unless you manage to triangulate." And she watched the blade move to other locations as I thought of different people.

"Think of me," said Tam, and as I did so nothing happened. "Must be faulty!" she said, smiling. And as I sat down once more Tam rose to her feet, and before I could respond touched my cheek, saying she needed to go.

*

Flukaggrrr, Hukrazz and Tansraw appeared late, about an hour after midday, and I was dozing in my chair.

They had been warned by the guards outside my door that I was sleeping but being in disgrace they still waited, milling around just outside the room, discussing whether they should knock on the door, and looking around they saw Hilda watching them.

"Good day, Hilda," said Tansraw, as he looked at her perched upon a run of the stairs. She watched, always silent, observing the two human guards, two orcs and one half-orc.

"Have you fucked His Lordship yet, or are you not so favoured?" She ignored him, and Flukaggrrr nudged Tansraw.

"She's a bloody hag," said Tansraw as if to reinforce his animosity.

"Leave her alone, you're in enough shit already."

"I was only wondering," said Tansraw, mumbling something about 'too skinny', before noticing with some concern that Hukrazz was knocking loudly on the door, a guard scowling at him, uncertain whether to intervene.

"Bloody idiot," said Flukaggrrr, who was also

caught off guard, "you might wake him up!"

"That's the idea, isn't it? And unlike you I'm not a turd, nor did I throw up over His Lordship like Tansraw."

"I didn't, you're inventing the story!" said Tansraw, somewhat self-doubting. "Oh shit! Did I really?"

"Yes," said both together.

One of the guards, smiling, looked at his fellow warder, muttering, "Idiot."

"Piss off! You useless human git," said Tansraw, still drunk and behaving badly. He pushed the guard backwards, none too gently.

One of the guards looked at Flukaggrrr. "Sort him out, sir, or I'll be forced to!" He rested his hand upon a small cudgel, and Flukaggrrr realising his own authority was being undermined by Tansraw's behaviour, grabbed Tansraw by the back of his neck and threw him to the ground. No mean feat as the half-orc was significantly taller.

"Game's over, Tansraw," said Flukaggrrr, just as one half of the doubled-leaved doors opened, and I, Miller, stood there surveying the situation.

I was not enamoured of either Flukaggrrr or Tansraw, and briefly looking at the two guards and noticing one raising his hand from a cudgel sack, a small bag of lead shot that hung by his belt used to club malefactors unconscious, and surveying the situation, Wisp bouncing of each mind in turn, I ahead of Wisp told the guards to place all three under arrest.

"Stick them in prison." My countenance stern, I was wrathful and angry, not the least I felt wretched, so desperately in need of sleep.

Flukaggrrr and especially Hukrazz appeared shocked. "Get into fucking line!" I shouted as the three stood in stunned silence.

Hukrazz was released within the hour, although the other two stayed longer, Tansraw doing obeisance as I looked at him through bars the following day, lying in shit and filth, no clean thresh for it was a prison, and he wallowed in turds and excrement, surrounded by rats and maggots, rotting remains of past half-consumed meals tossed at prisoners, no plates. It was after all meant to be a shit hole of discomfort.

As for Flukaggrrr, I was wroth, deeply disappointed. He who owed absolute obedience to me, the one whose life I had bought with too much silver, and, yes, I expected a lot, but no, not actually, for he owed everything to me and whilst a lifetime's debt is long, it wasn't without comfort. Indeed he had prestige, enjoying his authority in association with me, but I had been let down and that was unforgivable, an outrageous disgrace, at least that is how it felt.

"You stinking bastard. You who should never have allowed yourself to get pissed, too many drinks, and I had a bloody important guest!

"You were meant to guard me, not leave some drunken soak to throw up, caking me in vomit, whilst you slept with your whore!

"How do you propose to buy your life?" For I could afford to slay him, and the realisation was slowly dawning across his mind. No longer the prodigal son, allowed to misbehave.

Now, I understand that no hope of redemption is

as bad as no redemption, so I made a way back for him. He needed to have an escape clause, a way to regain favour; his misery would be a catalyst to propel him to better service, proper duty, and whilst in wrath I could have walked away with his corpse being thrown to dogs, it was probably not needed, or wise.

As the malefactions of the previous day's adventure with Tam subsided, I regained my wits yet was still incandescent with rage. *How could my men treat me with the beginnings of contempt? Shit. Grimnir was right, the best to guard were the men. And I doubted the building of a hybrid kingdom?* Although Hukrazz was innocent of charges, as the guards and Wisp reported. Still I was angry, furious.

This, the establishment of a kingdom, wasn't a game, and whilst I had secured a good start we needed to prepare for war!

*

Hilda came to me that day, a day after the moon was extinguished, and whilst I was wroth and despondent, she always had access, the guards at the door checking gently, making sure she carried no weapons. A pointless exercise for she was always searched, too often, but it was her lot and their responsibility.

Entering, she walked slowly across the stone floor, rugs covering a large section, keeping some of the chill from rising out of the flags, and I observed her entrance as I slouched over a table studying runes written upon vellum – my remembrance of how to action an aspect of craft that was too elusive and difficult to learn.

"Lord, I wish to worship in the woods outside Stours but Abroalt follows me around and restricts my association. I wish for more freedom."

Abroalt was a servant who was elderly and therefore safe, appointed to keep watch upon her and due to his senior years unlikely to make advances upon the young girl, tasked with keeping 'an eye'.

And she paused, seeking the right words, looking at the scrolls cast upon my table.

"He has no authority over you," I said, but raising my eyes I looked at her and noticed she had washed and cleansed herself, presenting herself in a wholesome manner, looking discreetly her best. She was fourteen, almost fifteen; we were of similar years, but I was now full grown, yet not she, for being human, pure blood, there were perhaps a couple more years for her.

She lowered her eyes, an unusual characteristic for she always held my gaze along with that of others.

"You never took me, even when I said I would be yours!"

"No," I said, with no support for her discussion. It was true that I had considered it, walking into her quarters and raping her; she had invited me but out of fear.

"So now I'm disparaged, and the likes of Tansraw insult. Even Berrek, your soldier, seeks to advance himself upon me." She spoke slowly, watching, eyes raised once more, studying with an intelligence that I wished more had.

"It is a weakness of mine, but I shall not readily

attack a woman." I looked back at the second parchment on the table. I wasn't shy, but simply trying not to forget a key point in my deliberations.

"Why?" she persisted, with a most argued of questions. And it was unexpected. "The whole world takes what it wants!"

"Because?" And I pondered the point. "It's wrong." It was a useless answer and I hadn't at that moment in time the wits to give a better one, yet thinking she deserved better, not the least I had slaughtered her father and had indeed dreamt of her… "I want my woman to be willing, not forced, nor obligated," and added, "you needed to ask twice."

"He wasn't my father, you know?"

"I didn't know that." And Wisp had been counselled to likewise leave her alone. I had a weakness towards the treatment of women, only ever knowing two; one the filthy, nasty, pug-faced mistress owned by and married to my former master, whose throat I'd slit, and Tam, who I admired. It was a charity, Tam having placed a lien on my conscience, and I wasn't a bully. Brutal yes, wicked perhaps, trying not to be. Women generally had such a shit existence, loving their children and husbands yet frequently treated cruelly, or dying in childbirth.

"I want to worship the old gods, in private, be left alone. Please tell Abroalt to stay away. I'm not welcomed in the woods if Abroalt follows me."

And I looked up at her.

"The old gods?"

"You know them as 'Grey', but they are ancient, of

the earth… Your woman knows."

"My woman?" And looking up again, my gaze temporarily averted, I didn't understand though the term 'Grey' rang a bell.

"The halfling."

"Tam?" And I slipped up, giving her name, disclosing by mistake the name of my visitor so that now I needed to learn and repair the damage, my lack of discretion. *Shit!*

"What relationship or understanding does Ta… the halfling have with you or your old gods?"

"You can call her Tam, I won't repeat the name," Hilda said, and I thought her far too bloody bright, and I was annoyed with myself. Still, it was probably best not to make an issue of it.

"You and Tam listen to the song, don't you? Do you think you were the first to hear it?"

And now she had my full attention. "Go on," I said as I pushed the scrolls together and reached for a tankard, half consumed, yet the ale was fresh, not stale.

"We meet in the woods, a glade, a few of us. We've always done so." And she faltered, worried she revealed too much. And as she said this Wisp knew my desire, permission given, and was studying her mind. "We respect the oldest of deities, now mostly forgotten."

And I was shocked for Wisp returned a moment later. *'She can cast craft, and I thought you were almost unique!'*

"No!" and I said it out loud.

"How the *by the abyss of hell, by Akrraatsy*, do you

cast spells?" And it was her turn to be dismayed, for she had assumed I knew nothing of the Grey Gods, so few had even heard of them, like some mythical religion, ancient, lost in antiquity. Nor for that matter had she given any clue as to her skills.

"I… I don't really, I… it's just… I'm just a novice. I like lying on the ground listening to sounds, being at one with nature, and life."

'Only half true,' said Wisp. *'She may be a novice, but she's not unskilled. I know she can, I saw the images in her head.'*

"Can you meditate and gather your magic in the earth's song?" And she looked at me, thinking carefully before answering.

"No, but I can hear it sometimes!" And she sat on the floor. "Our gift is granted through the spirits that dwell in all living things – trees, grass, roots, the water flowing down a hillside, all carrying the vitality and energy that permeates the world we live in.

"We gather slowly over many months. The forces of nature, the energy of life, found all around in the wind, the sun, all living things, even death simply returns that which is borrowed. We likewise borrow, honouring and revering that entrusted to us."

"And you have gathered a little while?" I questioned her, seeking knowledge, for knowledge was power, everything!

"A little while," she said, demurring, not a fulsome answer.

'Bollocks,' said Wisp. *'It might take an age, if you are to believe her? But she has energy.'*

"And what do you do with this energy?" I was fascinated by her answers, for my first meditation in the earth song had not been without a synergy of feeling to my surroundings.

"We heal the body and mind of those in need. Sometimes we try to..." And she faltered, and chose not to continue.

'Chance,' said Wisp. *'She tries to alter events.'*

"What else? You didn't finish your sentence."

"We try to heal mostly. Our gathered energies are only borrowed, there's nothing special, it's weak and gentle."

We talked for some time, and I didn't push her into answering or expanding upon that which I learnt, but I would raise the subject with Tam, for she had said there were no witches in the world, no familiars, no special black cats, yet this didn't seem so very dissimilar. I suspected her abilities were modest and not particularly harmful, like eating a peculiar mushroom and having visions of events yet to unfold.

"Do you wish me harm?" I asked a direct question, needing to know if her revelation placed me at risk, Wisp ready to read her hidden thoughts.

"No! I wish you to invite me to your bed." And she stared into my face. "Now I've asked you twice."

I laughed, not out of malice, but how she had said it plainly and without obfuscation, no coercion or obligation. And I thought I would need to bathe, though I didn't say it out loud, not wishing to belittle or undermine her spirit, her risk to life given generously.

CHAPTER 14

It had been my intention to take Isthmi, although rumours abounded that Urthing would be our 'next port of call' and I was behind on my reckless schedule, initially too ill to follow through on my plan to attack shortly after Tam had visited. Indeed plans had been put back, and then becoming somewhat enamoured of Hilda I became even less impatient and more distracted.

"We have about a hundred and seventeen men, plus twelve in training that I would call boys or farmers, not good enough nor nearly competent. They'd be slaughtered if we took them with us." Flukaggrrr was speaking to me some two weeks after Tam had left.

Listening to two of the town's councillors along with Flukaggrrr, Hukrazz and Tansraw it was reported that many families were seeking refuge amongst my town boundaries. True, we had better security and accordingly we always attracted people but the volume of new arrivals had leapt.

"There are rumours of goblins and fell men coming down from the mountains, driving farmers and woodsmen to find security." Stories of misery were filtering through; Hjalmar was ruling with an iron fist in Isthmi, driving people away.

"And the three spies sent to Isthmi? What report have they given?"

"It's been days since they left." Wisp had tried to visit the dreams of one of the spies and had been unable, believing at least one to be dead.

"There's no report, Lord, we should have heard back by now... No news, not good!"

Many matters were discussed, along with plans for defence whilst the main force was absent. The journey to Isthmi was some twenty-three miles, through woods and at least one sizeable forest – perfect terrain for my men, but goblins likewise.

"So Hjalmar's gathering a force, and no doubt he plans to attack us or Urthing himself." And as I watched, the men stood silent in front of me.

"We need to increase our force to one hundred and fifty, plus forty as militia, for the land must be protected should an opportunity to attack become available," I said.

"It'll take weeks to achieve, Lord," said Hukrazz, and one of the town's administrators added that there should be an increase in tax revenue for the town's population was growing significantly, especially if the tide of fleeing families didn't abate.

"So be it, we'll wait two months." And I wasn't too upset for Hilda was a serious distraction, not the least she looked much better naked than I had imagined.

*

Deep within his tower, a vanity in the small town of Isthmi for most of the buildings are hovels, with a few stone buildings owned by the wealthy – it's scarcely larger than a village, Hjalmar had been left alone, left alone from the infraction of deviants, protected by the rumours that he was a sorcerer of immense cunning and craft. He had been worried that the peasants below might rise up and rebel, for there had been talk of his blackmailing the local officials and gaining unfair advantages over the local population, all true.

Hjalmar, human, about five feet seven inches tall, medium build with thinning black hair cut short hasn't been idle. Dressed in sheepskins with small shrunken skulls hanging from his belt he looks down from his tower.

As a minor sorcerer in Edric's employ he had enlisted the support of the Avarti, though they now seemed somewhat eviscerated despite reassurances that a groundswell of people would follow Edric's cause. It seemed unlikely, indeed improbable, just a lie, yet now news had arrived and Edric commanded that he tolerated one of them.

Hjalmar had initially been enthused, awaiting a gift of servitude and goodwill, a chest containing gems that had failed to materialise, and now an effeminate, arrogant fop stood before him. Newly arrived, sent by craft, his Lord Edric apparently sees value in him and thus accordingly he, Hjalmar, needed to be more than disinterested.

A light mist and drizzling rain blows across the tower, some sixty feet tall, a building out of kilter with the surrounding structures. Grinning, he beckons the courtier diplomat to look down upon the town. The peasants below are all now in subjection, yet only two days prior he had worried for his safety. No longer was this an issue, not since two hundred goblins led by wild men passed the northern mountain range, driven from lands westwards in the lee of the mountains, allied with goblins that inhabited parts of the northern mountain passes, now all swearing fealty. More goblins were arriving and another one hundred men should arrive this week or the next, and the peasants of this small town would kneel before him.

"These ignorant bastards will be whipped into shape," he sneers, turning to the fop. "We will be attacking a neighbouring town called Stours; they're led by a half-orc sorcerer – intelligent apparently, a contradiction in terms you would have thought? Just as soon as you secure peace with the dwarves."

Patroal Irlaneson, Second Viscount of Skitol, peers over the edge, watching the townsfolk scurrying about their business, and having passed on his letters of introduction written by Edric, letters that commanded Hjalmar to provide a ten-man escort, he would be heading for the foothills of the dwarven realm, a distance in excess of a hundred miles, and he was worried for his comfort.

Still there were benefits, not the least that he would be well away from the wars; nor would he get too close to these foul goblins. He could see them corralled in a confined quarter of the small town, their stench drifting through the air. *Disgusting creatures.*

"I'll need clean men, and suitable transport," Patroal Irlaneson said, turning to Hjalmar. "Ambassadors need status, not a horse and cart."

"It's your job to keep the dwarves out of the fight." And smiling, Hjalmar added, "You'll look the part, don't worry."

*

"We will gather our men tomorrow evening. It's a full moon and the weather seems perfect but it'll take about three days; the wagons and baggage will slow us down." And as I sat there everyone paying attention, "I want to attack at midday, four days from now. Goblins, if there are any, dislike the sunshine." And pausing, I thought I was missing so much. "I want some of the newcomers interrogated."

So it was that learning of discourse and violence within Isthmi, we set off, two weeks later than planned; one hundred and twenty-eight men, plus a large number in baggage mules, women and scavengers, always more than you wanted, the women not wishing to leave their men yet raising morale, the warriors keen to impress, focussed on their task knowing their women watched.

Hilda was pregnant, and I was proud. She didn't show, yet women knew and I wondered how long she would keep her svelte appearance. A selfish thought for I enjoyed the shape she was, and if she was worried she didn't show it. I on the other hand was anxious, but women knew their business, and it gave her a status that she enjoyed.

Walking through a patchwork of light woodland copses interspersed with heather, couch grass and gorse, several horsemen were scouting ahead, the day fine and meeting no opposition this close to Stours. Berrek approached, a broad smile upon his face, looking like an idiot.

"That didn't take long." He grinned as he scratched his arse. "I thought you might have needed some lessons from me. I've known lots of girls and the best ones are those with rounded…"

"Do you think I'm interested in knowing how many women you've humped and infested with your filth?" I kicked him, deliberately missing. "Is whoring all you ever think about?" He looked at me as though I asked a trick question. "Also, leave Hilda alone." Not that he didn't already know she was out of bounds.

"Just a joke, Lord," he said, laughing. "I'm too busy anyway to give advice, but you could have watched and…"

"Sod off! Berrek, go and persecute someone else… do something useful." But actually I was in a cheerful mood. Yes, concerned about the battle ahead, but nonetheless liking the teasing the men gave me, a form of companionship and camaraderie, a respite from discipline, separation from the responsibilities of command.

Forty-four men had been left behind under the command of two sergeants, loyal men tasked with keeping Stours safe, but the most competent marched with me. A hundred and twenty-eight men seemed ample for the task in hand; even if we encountered stronger resistance than anticipated I was more worried about any acts of craft Edric's lieutenant, Hjalmar, might deploy.

In any event I had prepared a scroll that I was proud of, an illusion with some offensive characteristics, damned difficult to prepare and I had studied for hours fashioning the energy stored within the vellum. Not a permanent act of craft, but an incredible achievement; the men would be impressed and I was sure that it was far beyond the abilities of Hjalmar. This along with the craft stored within my body... I was formidable.

That night surrounded by a camp of nearly two hundred people, horses, wagons and the usual paraphernalia of travelling groups, the men and women were divided into smaller family units, each having their own fire. Sometimes groups would share. Hilda and I slept in the open, and I wished I'd brought a tent, still longing to strip her naked. I even considered wandering away from the men, but the ridicule would have been tremendous. A cheer would have ascended from the crowded camp, and I just knew it wasn't practicable, so I resigned myself to frustration, and slid a hand beneath her tunic, as she did likewise.

"What's that bloody smell?" I asked in the early hours of dawn, for there no doubt the camp stank of shit and waking early, the chill of the night still hung close to the ground, dew stuck like a thin misty veneer, such that Hilda's hair whilst not wet felt damp. "It smells like a cesspit."

"Not my hair I hope!" She smiled before wandering off to join a group of women gathering mushrooms, no doubt listening to stories of my injustices and poor decision making. Women could talk the hind legs off a donkey whilst having absolutely nothing of value to say. But given an opportunity to reach Their Lordships ear, via Hilda, she would hear all sorts of tales, some true, most not, all biased in the storyteller's favour. She was intelligent enough to realise.

"Have you shat next to my head?" I pointed at my nearest neighbour who looked a little hurt by the accusation.

"Not I, Lord. I shat over there." And he pointed somewhere closer to another man.

"Who no doubt shat somewhat over here." And looking around I realised the camp was riddled with shit, people defecating in the night. Indeed I was surrounded. "Bloody hell!"

*

"The scouts have seen smoke behind yonder hill Lord," a man said as he ran towards me.

"Don't tell me, tell Flukaggrrr." And being in a wood 'yonder hill' wasn't very descriptive. "Which hill?"

"There's a sizeable hill one mile beyond the wood's edge. And he pointed behind slightly to the west of where we stood. "He's with the patrol and I was told to report to you."

"How much smoke?" I asked, for it wasn't unusual in itself. Many woodsmen and hunters would be huddled around fires.

"A lot, Lord, perhaps a large gathering. Flukaggrrr's

gone to investigate."

Looking around the camp pitched under mature woodland trees, I thought our smoke might not be clearly discernible; there was a chance at least. I ordered the fires extinguished, and whilst some resisted I repeated my order three minutes later. Some women complained about half-cooked food going to waste.

I ordered the camp to prepare to depart, the men to the front, and we advanced slowly through the wood, a distance of four hundred yards, edging closer towards the woodland edge.

Wisp knew Flukaggrrr, and whilst he couldn't read his thoughts unless in conversation with me or at night when he dreamt, he nonetheless could see what Flukaggrrr could see, and he was tasked with reporting back.

Drawing my sword, I knew in which direction to send Wisp, for the blade tugged at my hand as I thought of him.

Wisp returned as my men became organised, Hukrazz giving commands, men understanding not to disobey, and as I walked to the front approaching the edge of the wood before me, there stood a small hill, perhaps half a mile wide, three hundred feet tall, with a flattened grass-covered summit, trees growing along the southern edge.

'You'll love this,' said Wisp. *'It's your favourite religion, I've seen the toggles, with a man you've met before. Eighty approximately, inclusive of women and children. I'm going back to listen, I can observe.'*

I didn't hinder Wisp, and as we waited on the edge of the wood I decided to split my men into four parts;

one to remain with the women, one to mount the hill and the remaining two groups to divide either side of the hill. But we waited for Flukaggrrr to return.

Twenty minutes later, "You're well concealed, Lord," said Flukaggrrr as he dismounted and sought me out, walking over with several women gathering the horses and leading them to the rear.

"There's a large group of men and families, perhaps ten proper soldiers, though I suspect they might swell that number to thirty. They seem to be travelling either towards Isthmi or Urthing, not Stours, and there's an important well-dressed man amongst them, ordering people about, but he doesn't look like a soldier, maybe a priest. I don't know."

"I'll know more in a minute or two." And looking at Flukaggrrr, I muttered, "Craft!"

"Don't know why I bother, Lord, you seem to find everything out!" he said, not churlishly but I thought it an unnecessary comment and inappropriate.

Wisp having reported back, I retained my initial arrangement, keeping the soldiers divided into four, Tansraw leading the middle over the hill, Flukaggrrr and myself each taking a wing, and Hukrazz left behind to look after the camp, much to his annoyance.

"Next time, Lord, I'll throw up over you. Perhaps I will be rewarded with shit shovelling! Or some higher duty." I had had enough of this gradual erosion of discipline, of disrespect to my authority, and grabbing Hukrazz by his tunic I dragged him fifty yards aside, and swore at him.

"You fucking miserable bastard." And I was angry, for I had kept Hukrazz back not because he was disloyal, but the opposite – he was good, bloody competent, and intelligent.

"You ignorant orc bastard." I was cross and pissed off. "My woman is here and I wanted you to look after her, not Tansraw, not someone else, but you." And he looked up at me, perhaps realising that it wasn't the slight that he had perceived it to be.

"Sorry Lord, I just… just wanted the responsibility and right to fight… I meant no disrespect."

And I, having made my point, yet far enough away from Tansraw, allowed my wrath to subside. "You have the greatest of responsibility – my unborn child, my woman, my property."

Men saw my anger, some heard parts of the conversation, but Tansraw's name was growled deeply yet not loudly.

A few more words, some to emolliate, and Hukrazz and I rejoined the other three leading men, and we set off, for I hated the Avarti. Their treachery and Grimnir's near assassination were forefront in my mind.

'You know the one, the man you met in the Avarti house, in Cragtor? When you were taking notes with Glamdrun, the one with the fake address?' but I couldn't picture him, and relying upon Wisp's assurance we marched the three groups destined to meet in half an hour's time, the left and right axis slanted northwards as to remove any chance of the 'enemies" retreat.

It was two hours after dawn, perhaps an hour and a quarter after sunrise, and as I stood in front of the Avarti camp, some thirty-two men under my command, I watched as women and children ran to the centre, soldiers gathering weapons, some cries of dismay, as a line of some forty men gathered, wielding makeshift weapons – many with swords yet too many with daggers or clubs looking nervously at me, worried, for whilst they outnumbered us it was clear that we were warriors to a man. No makeshift instruments of death lay in our hands; each of my men carried swords and not a few had bows, arrows nocked, swords in sheaves or slung over shoulders, and all my men had armour, not chain like myself, but studded jerkins or better.

A man, tall and well dressed, was encouraged to treat with us, and as he was pushed to the front, I part recognised him and he, unsure and unprepared, brushed down his clothes, steadied his nerves gaining an outward appearance of calm, and walked slightly forwards. His voice was controlled, relying upon his skill in words, a diplomat tasked with diffusing an unpleasant situation.

"Warriors, we greet you in friendship." And it was more the sound of his voice that I recognised, for when I had visited the Avarti house, it had been under the illumination of lamps that added nothing to my dark vision.

Did he recognise me? I didn't know, at least at that point, for whilst I was dressed in mail as I had been when entering the house, circumstance can distract the mind.

"You are outnumbered and will drop your weapons and submit, for you trespass upon my lands and haven't done obeisance."

"Obeisance is something every lord should

demand, and we withhold it not, yet to which noble warrior do I speak?" And he shuffled slightly, continuing, "Just so I might behave correctly."

"All bollocks!" I mumbled. "He utters clever meaningless noise." It sounded good, addressing his enemy with tact and manners.

"For I have no ill will against you," he continued, "and whilst injury to either party is not that which we seek it would seem the odds are sadly too close." And with the utmost reasonableness, "May we not pass in peace? There is no intent on our part to do otherwise."

I didn't know his name, nor was I seduced and influenced by his words, for despite the reasonableness of his speech a fire of hatred burnt within my heart. True, I had met this man before, yet of his transgressions against Tam I knew nothing, nor his rank and betrayal of the King of Culanun. He was of the Avarti, it was enough.

And as we parleyed Tansraw's men appeared atop the hill, walking down in line, Flukaggrrr yet to appear.

"I am the Lord of Stours and you will yield, dropping your weapons." And as if to reinforce the hopelessness of their plight, Flukaggrrr appeared somewhat to their rear and behind; strung out too thinly, yet they were facing me and should they turn and face Flukaggrrr's slender line, I would charge. Tansraw would no doubt seek his advantage and attack their exposed quarter.

"Got the bastards!"

Flukaggrrr ordered his men to constrict, all the time advancing, tightening his thin line, as my men likewise spread out very slightly, not too much, and Tansraw advanced down the hill, not to the bottom, still keeping his advantage of height. A job well done, for Tansraw could have made an error but didn't.

"Lord, we will pay our tithes, our dues, we mean no transgression against you." And the worm started looking around seeking any secondary option, that is, a means of escape, an opportunity to flee should fighting erupt. If necessary his brethren could be sacrificed for the greater 'good' – his greater good!

And now it was my turn as women screamed within their camp, realising their position was dire, no means of escape, surrounded by warriors on all sides.

"If he speaks for all of you, you may die sound in the knowledge that you didn't... weren't given the opportunity to surrender... but if he doesn't control you, or lead you... then now is your one chance to submit. Lay down your weapons and kneel!"

And as I walked forwards, I replaced my sword and took hold of my axe, in both hands, an instrument of slaughter.

"Your chance is almost up." And as my words carried across the line of men, a few started to drop their weapons, not all, but it became a ripple, as men, realising their comrades were giving in, kneeled, weapons cast in front as acts of obeisance, contrition, persuading their peers to do likewise.

I slew almost all of them, sparing five young mothers and their children plus five other men who I deemed not devotees of Avart. The rest died, bound with hands behind their backs, although it took me until midday to learn what I could, examining most with Wisp's help whilst Flukaggrrr collected and sorted the wealth, bellowing discipline, seeking to thwart thievery and jealousy amongst my own men.

At the same time as minimising thievery we made sure we knew where all the Avarti's wealth was hidden and secured eight wagons and ponies, plus a significant amount of silver, swords, weapons and useful merchandise.

Patroal Irlaneson watched as his own men were killed first, not of the Avarti, but clearly warriors from Isthmi under the command of the courtier, and as I questioned the rest as to their obedience to their petty god, Wisp helping all along, he looked on in horror as I with cruelty ordered the slaying of his brethren.

He had only joined their company the previous night, having stumbled across them, delighted to greet his fellow worshippers, encouraging them to travel to Urthing as Isthmi wasn't wholesome, riddled with foul goblins and wicked men.

Looking back upon that confrontation, as I sit upon my wooden throne, I wish I'd known of Patroal Irlaneson's treachery, for he was spared... A worm obviously, but a guest in Tam's fortress? Who'd stolen from her! Had I known at that time, I would have disembowelled him slowly. As it was, he was cruelly beaten, but kept alive for questioning.

I made an offer to the few women, children and men I'd spared, to either take one wagon and head to Urthing, although the journey wouldn't be safe, or travel to Stours which they could easily achieve without fear of attack.

They were mostly in shock, and didn't really know

what to do, so I sent them to Stours without any weapons, but allowed them to keep their own possessions, and some silver, for these few were in my opinion mostly innocents. Yet I told them that if they ever associate with the Avarti, they would suffer the same consequences as the others.

Some of my men were dismayed at my brutality, others happy to have a part in the violence.

As for me, I needed to distract the men; needed to maintain discipline and awe. I had been too wrapped in comfort, not walking with the soldiers enough, humping my woman, and the men had grown complacent with their wealth and daily pay.

Five hours after sunrise, the day turning past noon, I lined the men up and placed a spoil before them, a heap of silver, a tiny amount of gold along with heirlooms of the dead, precious possessions beautifully made, carried across the mountains by the Avarti, whose bodies were now piled upon a pyre, the flames lit half an hour before and only now licking the bodies. Clothing and hair were the first to ignite yet dying back as the greater branches within the bonfire took hold, fat ready to drip down and flagrate, adding support to struggling flames.

"These are the spoils." And I stood in front of my men, wrathful for I knew more than a few had stolen and withheld plunder.

"Every man who has stolen and withheld wealth from me," and I looked at them, telling some on the sides to move closer, *"will die if they do not now add all that they have taken.*

"It shall forgive you, but to disobey me is death.

To fight and obey is your duty, for I pay that you serve, *me*."

I was pissed off for I had witnessed growing disobedience and was keen to reassert my authority in a brutal manner. I would slaughter and make an example, though I was disappointed I needed to.

Three men added stolen silver, one dropping a ring he had stolen, but Wisp was enjoying the prospect of death. *'It's fascinating when a man dies, their mind becomes a hollow and it—'*

'Shut up and search!'

I ask the three each on the end if they have stolen, and coming to the fourth, he was caught, not having cast his spoils into the heap, and dragging him forward, a man, not an orc, I kicked him to the floor, before reaching amongst his tunic and pulling out a pouch of silver concealed upon his body.

I in silence cast a missile that struck his head and screaming he rolled in agony, before I drew my knife and slit his throat.

"He may have been your friend, and a valiant man, but anyone who steals from me will rue this day. He's no friend of mine, nor your fellows beside."

You could hear items falling to the floor as men hustled sideways, disowning contraband stolen, items let fall, landing next to them, their neighbour not chastising.

"Have you stolen?" And I walked around the men, Wisp reading the reply of each I questioned, searching and confirming the veracity of their replies.

"Not me."

"Nor I," said each in turn.

"I've nothing on my person." Yet alongside many, scattered on the floor was a considerable wealth.

"Don't lie to His Lordship, he is a sorcerer of tremendous power yet he's fair and decent. You and I owe him our lives and future. Your families and children are blessed, we benefit from his rulership; he's our lord, our champion. Any bastard that steals from him steals from us all."

And Gwynnru joined Flukaggrrr, stepping forward to support my authority. "Any shit who has stolen from our Lord Miller, will be a traitor amongst us. Don't fuck your future, hand it over, cast it upon the ground... You miserable bastards... We all get paid, and probably rewarded, even if we don't you owe him your fealty." And Gwynnru, reckless in devotion risked a little siding with me so strongly, though still he lacked the high intelligence that I sought.

Not pleased that 'Miller' was used but assured of Gwynnru's loyalty, it was a good speech, and really I needed to stop being sensitive, for Gwynnru had been proud to call his child after my name. I didn't know how far advanced his woman was, nor indeed if it was a male child.

So the wealth of that day was piled high; seven thousand in silver or so I reckoned.

"Half is mine." And the remaining portion was divided between four groups, each gaining twenty-one silver pieces per man.

I kept the bulky items, easier to split the remainder amongst the men, some of whom came and knelt before me. Not needed, but they felt partly guilty, wishing to reaffirm their devotion. Twenty-one silver pieces was a good reward.

Indeed Hukrazz likewise was not disappointed as each of his men, many complaining that they were disparaged, citing weak association with me, and he because of it would fail to include them in the opportunities that might unfold. Yet they were surprised, for I made sure that Hukrazz's authority was not undermined. He and I walked amongst his men reinforcing his status, claiming Hukrazz was their lieutenant and had secured equal pay for all of them. Silver was handed by Hukrazz to each man in turn.

"Hukrazz, these are now your men." And I took Flukaggrrr aside, determined that forty or so, a manageable group, would become my unit of competence, each under a commander that I could trust, divisible and manageable. No group too large that they might individually subvert my authority.

It had been an easy victory, and I summoned Hukrazz, Gwynnru, Flukaggrrr and Tansraw and gave each a bonus from my own funds. Gwynnru was not a lieutenant but was blessed that day.

Indeed I changed the rules. Gwynnru, although lacking intelligence was allowed to command my bodyguard. Not so many men, for he was not skilled in authority, not naturally gifted in the subtleties of command, but ten was a number he could cope with, and his loyalty was without doubt.

*

Berrek, the miserable turd, now assigned to Tansraw's unit had left a pile of silver at his feet, and I had noticed. So summoned separately as the camp made ready to depart, I called Tansraw to attend.

Berrek grovelled in the forest floor, head and nose buried in the fallen vegetation. "You're lucky to be alive," I said, furious with his lack of integrity.

He looked at me, and pled his innocence as Wisp confirmed the lie. "Stupid bastard! Do it again, Berrek, and you'll be back to licking Grabbarzz's arse, even if you have to dig him up to do so!"

Patroal Irlaneson had with incredible skill squealed like a boar trapped in a noose, yet with silken words slippery as an eel, he tried to dissuade me that his mission was other than peaceful, a misdirection cast with the skill of a huntsman seeking to hide his intent from the deer he stalked, as pilgrims travelling to preach peace in a world riven by violence.

In the end, vomiting, retching as he was led past his slaughtered brethren, not seeing the few I had saved, he relented and gave every scrap of information that I thought to ask. I learnt of plans of the twenty guards at Isthmi reinforced by goblins and the arrival of more than one hundred wild men from the western mountainside. The attempt to placate the dwarves and Hjalmar's plan to attack Stours.

Patroal Irlaneson, bound and convinced that he was likewise to die was taken prisoner, and secured amongst the women trussed up on a cart, for I wanted to learn more from him, sure in the knowledge that he had so much more useful information than I could procure in the given time allowed.

One thing was immediately clear, I needed to capture Isthmi swiftly. Time was pressing.

CHAPTER 15

We approached more carefully than I might have
originally planned, yet with a swiftness nonetheless,
we travelled for two more days, worried that one
hundred plus men would be reinforcing their ranks
before we had time to take the town, losing an
advantage of surprise and skill at arms. Goblins and
townsfolk would be hard yet not impossible to
overcome.

I wasn't worried by goblins, but the men? My men
might be overawed by the numbers, and we slew
patrols as we approached, allowing none to escape,
this in itself a warning to Isthmi and Hjalmar,
although I doubted he had full co-operation within
the small town.

Wisp went ahead, limited in what he might learn,
unable to read thoughts but better than a blind scout,
and arriving at a small hill situated before their
southern gate, having swung round during the final

night we gathered at the far side. Only three fires amongst the whole camp were allowed to be lit, for I wished no illumination in the night sky; no need to forewarn.

The next day, uncomfortable for it had rained during the night, the men cold and very few having slept, we advanced to the top of the hill. The wagons and general baggage train were stationed securely as my men advanced downwards, overcoming with ease a last small patrol who for the most part seeing warriors approaching fled towards the gates, one horn sounding, though we were visible to the men watching stationed within the town and I thought to advance on my own, casting an act of craft upon the watchers stationed on the ramparts. These soldiers of Isthmi stood watching as we approached, reliant upon their stout defences, defiant, behind a wall of wooden spikes and barricades.

In the end it wasn't necessary for before my horn and cries, there issued a force of four hundred goblins, far more than I had been led to believe, and shouting that they should rise up and overthrow their wicked and disgusting master, it mattered not, my words lost, drowned out by the din and shouts of these disgusting creatures.

The numbers were far in excess of the information obtained, yet surely they must have been newly arrived for my questioning of the Avarti had been thorough.

"They're maggots upon the face of the earth. Each of you will find it easy to slay them." And as if in proof I ordered that my archers form in front of the main body of men and launch a shower of missiles, raining down upon the shrieking horde, as we ourselves edged forwards, not quite leaving our elevated position.

Thus began a battle I wasn't wanting, too difficult, for whilst I didn't doubt my own ability to slaughter these creatures, there were far too many. I worried for the hearts of my quaking men.

"Hold to your courage, we shall have the victory." And seeing ten or more fall before our arrows, I spoke many more words of encouragement as the foul creatures swarmed up the hill, my men charging downwards, seeking the momentum and advantage of height, also wishing to place a distance between the enemy and their women and baggage train.

Flukaggrrr stood next to me as I cast a spell carefully prepared beforehand, an act of craft that I had studied long before and placed upon a vellum scroll; vellum so it didn't crack.

"Uh, wow! What the fuck's that? It's not from around here, that's for sure!" Flukaggrrr knew my spells were sometimes illusionary, and not as lethal as they seemed.

"It's a horse of course, a creature from hell," I said, slowly for I was studying this act of craft and didn't want to lose sight completely and break my tentative concentration upon it.

And forming, ascending from the ground one hundred yards in front or our men, and perhaps fifty from the enemy, both sides hesitated as a hideous apparition, smelling foul, and now fully formed, galloped towards the enemy line.

"Really? It looks like a five-legged mule with an

arse raised into the air ready to be humped. Does it want to fornicate with the enemy? Why has it got five legs?"

"There's only four legs and a tail, and it sounds like a horse," I said, for in truth it wasn't the closest resemblance I'd hope to achieve.

"It does, Lord? Like a horse in despair, having been celibate for three years it's granted access to an ugly donkey that's playing 'hard to get'!" And he continued in laughter, "But yes, it does if I cover my ears and stand on yonder hill. If I pretend the fifth leg's a tail… it vaguely resembles a horse."

And as I ignored him, sending the illusionary animal towards the enemy, Flukaggrrr added, "Does it do anything other than bewilder the goblins? That and make them roll around laughing?"

"Watch!" And as the strange creature caused considerable consternation amongst the opposing ranks, indeed they thinned out from before its advance, yet not too fearful, it emitted a fart, so loud as to cause Flukaggrrr to laugh again, only louder, that is, until many of the enemy started retching, falling to their knees, or standing coughing and wheezing.

"It was difficult to create… you have no idea." And as I said those words Flukaggrrr, sensing the advantage, encouraged his unit not to tarry.

"Kill the bastards!" he cried. "Come on, Tansraw, Hukrazz, get your men fighting!"

I could see into Isthmi, espying a man atop a tower, peering towards the battle, and pointing him out to Wisp, I commanded that he visit and 'know' my enemy.

I ran down the hill, the illusionary animal no longer under my concentration, 'galloping' at the rear of the hoard of goblins not near my men, but still a worry for the goblins, their leaders, orcs and men commanding, struggling to keep their foul ranks in order.

Flukaggrrr's men formed a line now close to the enemy who if anything wanted to advance, shaken yet massively outnumbering our men, seeking to climb the hill and place a distance between themselves and the phantom from hell.

Two explosive flames were cast amongst their ranks, the fire consuming a total of fifty goblins, my last acts of craft save two – a portal spell that I held in reserve, and an enlargement, an act of craft that added to my height, strength, deepening my voice, for a short while.

My men, led by Hukrazz sought the advantage, pressing against the void left by screaming goblins, their thin armour made from animal hide, their hair and clothing on fire; not a magical fire, for the flames whilst caused by magic were now real enough, and as they in agony fled hither and thither, burning, considerable confusion was caused amongst their own ranks.

We pressed on as I drew my axe and charged to the edge of their ascending ranks, exposed, and screaming hatred and death. I was a lord of war, oblivious to danger, assaulting their flank. Those unfortunates would rather have fought anyone but me.

Six arrows missed as I ran bellowing and cursing, the joy of battle filling my heart, dispelling anxiety.

The chaos of war allows for little understanding of other events. Concentrating on the task in hand I was the harbinger of death and I drove into their side, slaughtering an orc with my axe sweeping down, not cleaving the orc in half, but with one cruel blow I had taken one of their commanders. He for his part had sought to encourage the goblins, hoping to parry the swing. You cannot parry a two-handed axe, yet he had essayed, nonetheless.

Never let your enemy dictate the terms of battle, neither that of an army as a whole or singularly in hand-to-hand combat.

Not being in rank or constrained by orders, I was at liberty to run, seeking my own ground, immune to the darts that sought to slay me, and I cut a swathe through their side. Killing twenty, the shaft of my axe, the haft wrapped in course, rough-bound leather assisted my grip; such a little thing. A hoop made of thinly wrapped leather halfway up the shaft was designed so that the blood running down, given by the fallen, would drip to the floor allowing my hands to remain mostly dry, my grip not slippery.

Yet I needed to see the battle and whilst the joy of killing was surging through my body, my mind acknowledging no fatigue, I peeled leftwards, ascending slightly, cutting into terrified goblins, who casting glances behind knew I was closing upon them. One glanced nervously towards me, then another as goblin upon goblin shied away. I advanced through their ranks, the axe blade swinging violently, whistling through the air, slicing at any opportune moment.

The victory was ours for the goblins, a faithless and ignoble race of creatures, had now lost about a hundred of their own numbers, mostly through my craft, and being essentially cowardly bullies, some at the rear and sides started to hesitate, a few simply running; not the majority, true, but the beginnings of capitulation.

We for our part had lost six – three to arrows, three in combat and perhaps a further eight injured, but fighting on, indeed I included myself in the eight for I had been stabbed in the back, the blade twisting in the hands of a man who had not increased the force of his thrust, never being taught how to overcome chain armour, the blade partly penetrating, a quarter of an inch, thrusting links aside, not enough to slow me down. He had died, for I'd certainly noticed him, my axe slicing his nose off as he leant backwards trying to avoid my strike, yet his belly trimmed as a slice of gut was cleaved from his body, nose and gut entrails falling to the floor.

And then as our numbers too few sought to maximise and deny the enemy retreat, we were attacked on the side. Ninety to a hundred wild men coming late to battle drove upon our flank, turning certain victory into despair.

The battle so nearly won was becoming desperate, too many, too few men, too miserable was our position, for having sought to maximise the victory we had no spare to wield and counter the new enemy arriving north-westward.

Defeat was staring me in the face, and I ran alone to hinder the enemy; no hope, but still we fought.

"Hilda's casting a spell!" cried Flukaggrrr. "You miserable bastard of a half-orc. But I'll die alongside you," and he looked at me, screaming in my face, "and every time I see you in hell, I'll remind you what a turd you are!" But it wasn't said with venom, merely the freeness of speech that comes with those destined to die, uttered in combat, men resigned and reflecting on their fate, consigned to die as brothers.

"No! Really?" And as I looked back I could see her on her knees, arms outstretched, eyes closed, though it was hard to be certain.

My blood ran cold; I was buggered for already exhausted and stretched, I had spent my energy. What act of craft could my gentle Hilda do? My limbs ached, I was exhausted; the realisation of defeat so long denied was becoming reconciled in my mind. No hope, only despair.

All the words of valour spoken to my men, a conceit, words uttered, speeches given of a day the enemy would lose. How our victory would be acknowledged by our forebears and celebrated by out descendants, words given to shore up quaking hearts and now becoming unbelievable.

Wisp silent, the doom of finality reached my heart. No hope, all options cast already, the battle turning against my men, and they, shrieking, sped past as they fled, running away, looking to their lord, but no succour was forthcoming.

The enemy sensing the slaughter ran forward, their hearts reinforced, for when an army breaks, and it was as army in those parts, the massacre becomes complete, men slain as they beg for clemency, hoping against hope for some charity that is elusive, none ever given.

I drew my sword, casting my axe to the ground and being fey in heart and spirit, I readied my stand, yet not a stand, for I would choose the way of my death, and I sped forwards certain of my ill fortune. Exhausted, yes. Incandescent with rage? Certainly! There would be no cowering, no shitting of my britches. *Let no one forget my valour. Sod the world.*

And then it happened, or rather nothing did, but I guess it was this time, for men striking wild as they ran away, gained success... A backwards thrust as an enemy goblin charged becoming fortunate, their chance swing gaining a devastating strike, and yet men still ran, alive, unexpectedly, and I ran screaming, releasing my spirit, letting the gods know I was to be expected. Fey and reckless, determined in death to be obstinate, pig-headed. No surrender, no quarter gifted.

My lungs bellowing a battle cry, heart labouring, pumping blood through my veins oblivious to the dangers, already resigned to defeat, and to my left five of my men formed a defensive ring and were proving difficult to slay.

The bloodlust heaving war within my veins, I, despising the desperation of the hour, found a grim delight in the manner of my death. How many could I take with me? No song to be sung about my valour, but at least in this I would bear witness, informing the gods that I was no worm or coward.

Goblins and men died before my feet, each cut successful, each counter gaining an unexpected advantage, every sword stroke winning the maximum opportunity, and as I watched, or rather noticed, I was leaving a trail of devastation.

Half my force of men, perhaps sixty, were fleeing or dead and injured, yet most simply in flight, but the others as of champions of old were gathering their heart, finding skill where none had existed before, and the enemy still enthused, still sure of victory came on. Wave upon wave, crashing against an indomitable granite wall of stalwart men, orc and those of mixed blood.

There upon that battlefield camaraderie was forged; in those desperate hours, trespasses against each other were forgiven, and deeds of valour would later be recounted whilst drowning far too many ales, yet no man would strike their neighbour, sworn enemies fighting together not seeking revenge, for all were brothers, blood feuds forgiven, not forgotten, but so great was the spirit forged in the face of death, that each neighbour's past transgressions were ignored. 'Friendships forged upon the battlefield are difficult to deny, despite family feuds.' How is any blood feud to be scored when your bastard neighbour defends your body, cutting an enemy down before they impale you?

The steel fortress of my men wielding swords, knives and hammers, indeed any instrument of infraction, sought to fight to the last, hearts emboldened, and the enemy not understanding the tide was turning came upon my men, sure of their victory.

A number of the able bodied that had initially fled, tarried, looking back, not totally devoid of valour but not wanting to risk their less perilous position, watched for a while, waiting... talking amongst themselves, seeking the elusive courage that is reinforced through numbers, hoping for reassuring words from each other. Yet they observed impossible odds.

A few women, led by one, I didn't know her name, formed a narrow line about the hill and raising bows, with less strength than a man might draw but with courage no less than the greatest of heroes, launched flight after flight of deadly strikes, seeking the bowels of the enemy. These women, the property of their men, determined not to be parted, yet having a heart that could not be quelled, desperate to aid their loved ones.

Arrow after arrow was loosed, round upon round falling into the thicket of the enemy ranks, many goblins falling as arrowheads pierced their animal hide armour and flesh.

I almost wept later (no I didn't) hearing of their courage, for a flank of the enemy attacked the women, driving into their side, such that their thin line gave little resistance. Too many were slaughtered. Yet the men fallen to the rear, seeing an opportunity of valour came to their women's aid and drove the assault away, likewise winning the moment, unexpectedly! And having secured a minor victory, fortified in heart, thirty-eight or so seeing the incredible resolve and resolution of their peers charged, driving once more down the hill to rejoin the affray.

Later, five days after the battle these women who risked so much and showed greater determination than so many others were honoured, much to the embarrassment of my men.

I, indignant, risked the wrath and fury of those who were ashamed to listen, rounding upon any that looked away or muttered in the crowd. The townsfolk forced to hear as I praised *all* the champions of that day, women included.

So it was, unexpectedly, that the goblins, along with the men and orcs that led them, some five hundred, were defeated, at a cost of thirty-nine of my men – decent, honest soldiers, who should have gone home and seen their families.

I was pissed. Not drunk – pissed off. I wouldn't allow any to flatter me, for although I had killed swathes of the vile creatures and ultimately won the day, it was after all no more than my obligation and duty, also my wounds would be tended whilst others would groan in agony, wise women tending as best they could as families of the fallen wallowed in anguish and misery.

My plan to capture the large village of Isthmi had almost failed. I had suffered a victory but in my scheming it was almost a crushing defeat, for the men would take weeks to recover their heart and I couldn't blame them.

CHAPTER 16

The battle before Isthmi had ended with the last of the goblins scurrying within the small town as the gates were shut, some twenty or so of their comrades left to die outside, falling to their knees or running away, pursued by orcs – my orcs, who can run incredibly swiftly with immense stamina. I cared nothing for the enemy's fate, neither did I question blood upon jowls, for I'm sure the animalistic brutality of my orcs' hunting had been slow in slaking.

No cheers, no goading, for there were no songs sung whilst the enemy still lived, yet both Hjalmar and I were now aware of each other. It was only midday, and I bellowed over the ramparts whilst my men stayed some two hundred yards away, capable of seeing any dart fired at them, dodging the odd missile, yet most were fired at me, all to no avail, for my ring provided protection.

'Where is he, Wisp?' There would be no peace. There

could be none.

'He's inside, readying to read a scroll. It's a very large scroll, and he's panicking.'

"Gwynnru and Flukaggrrr, Tansraw, Hukrazz, to me now. Run."

But Tansraw couldn't run, being badly injured. A man stood in his place. "He's injured, Lord, and has sent me."

"Flukaggrrr, I want those gates broken down. I'm going to kill the bastard, yet I cannot escape." Looking at Flukaggrrr, I judged his heart. "I'm going in by craft and you must now rescue me." I was apoplectic, worried that the scroll he was studying might lead to his escape.

Furious, indignant that the blood of my men, my warriors, my women, my champions might be shed without the complete victory they deserved.

"There's no way this bastard's going to escape." I said the words out loud and Wisp, knowing my mind, not needing to listen to spoken instruction was silent, for he was going to reinforce my thoughts, guide my craft done so many times before yet never when my emotions were raging this strongly, at least not in the manner of portal travel. Nonetheless, I'd seen the balcony; it was within safe portal range and was confident.

I grabbed Gwynnru and Kyle, Tansraw's man, by the neck, and looking at Kyle, said, "We have more slaughtering to do," and with my mind concentrating, reinforced by Wisp such that I was certain of success, I uttered words of craft, the last of my power save one.

We vanished.

The balcony was slender, some five feet wide and sixty feet from the ground, and I with only my sword and two companions arrived somewhat squashed between the stone balustrade, and the main body of the tower.

None tarried or questioned their location, as under my instruction we sought a door and to Kyle's credit and that of Gwynnru's too, they, so filled with the fever of battle, did not quailed or shy from following me, not understanding other than they were there, and now here, a great act of sorcery, yet alive. Death having only half an hour ago been so certain, and now this magic a small terror paling into insignificance amongst the terrors of the day.

"Good men." Said without condescension, looking at the pair of them. "Draw your daggers and swords, and slay everyone before us. No permission required!"

A wooden door, iron studded and bound with strips of metal was found set back slightly in the wall, for like a round stone windmill this tower had immensely thick walls and looking up and seeing the walls tapering inwards, I wondered if indeed this building was simply a converted mill.

Kyle grabbed a large iron ring that when turned lifted the internal sneck. The door unlocked for whilst there was a securing bolt it hadn't been deployed.

As we entered, there was a sudden difference in temperature, indeed the noise from outside was almost muted. A warmth and silence enveloped us along with the scent of burning incense. Rugs covered parts of great wooden beams that spanned the floor; a huge oak cog still in situ hung from roof timbers.

"Careful where you tread, there will be trap doors – beware of the rugs." Though I later found out that my caution was misplaced for whilst there were indeed trapdoors, they had long since been secured.

Sword in hand, aware that the change in air pressure had probably forewarned of our presence, I thought of the man I had seen watching us from afar, and I sensed my sword give the weakest of tugs, upwards above my head and to my right.

"Upstairs." And there, wrapping around the side of the internal wall, a wooden stairway with no balustrade fashioned after the mill had been converted.

With no desire to tarry, my back aching, my men coming to terms with the dreadful events of the day, a worm, a maggot upstairs! Probably nearly finished reading his scroll, and so in need of being slaughtered.

Roaring as I ran for the stairs, screaming murder, yes, giving warning of my approach, but sorcerers aren't warriors and I wanted at the very least to make him stumble over his lines, risk of my injury be damned. I'd gut the bastard.

There he was, hands shaking as he stared at his scroll, unable to complete the arcane words written, and as he glanced at me, dropping the parchment from his hand he uttered words that would hurt.

A magical dart, powerful yet only one, singularly struck me in my chest. He could have done so much better – my mouth, my head, my genitals, no fucking imagination! Yet such was the fire of battle still burning within my heart, despite being struck a horrendous blow I managed to clear the top of the stairs and as my mind reeled, shocked by the infraction upon my body, I thrust my sword towards him, catching him successfully, the last blessing of Hilda's spell.

I was nonetheless felled, kneeling, my body screaming in pain, my heart labouring, its muscles constricting and pumping blood beyond that which it was designed to manage. I watched as Gwynnru ran forward and pierced Hjalmar in the stomach, and tugging with the proficiency of a warrior used to extracting a blade, stabbing again, before striking down upon his neck and shoulder.

Hjalmar was dead, but I was in no fit state to continue. The magical dart had not cut my body, and my armour had offered little protection against the energy. Accordingly I was in considerable distress, a situation I expected to last many hours.

Kyle and Gwynnru cast Hjalmar's body over the parapet, and with my support made a deal with the wildmen; their freedom if they slaughtered the remaining forty or so goblins, the townsfolk helping with surprising alacrity.

In all the misery of death and treachery, thinking the worst was over, words were uttered to me by Wisp, for my men had worried, unable to advise. News came to me... calamitous, dreadful... Hilda had been wounded, stabbed during the enemy's assault upon the women's flank. Patroal Irlaneson had broken his bonds and with malice, seeking revenge, had sought to slay my woman and unborn child in the confusion of battle.

I had no power of craft to heal, nor shaking and sweating in agony did I have the wherewithal to assist.

I never cry, but my soul can, and being carried surrounded by Gwynnru and four of his men, and lying next to Hilda, I saw how grievous her wound. She lay in distress, my plight inconsequential to her pain.

"My dear lord, I have no power left," she said as she sweated beads of perspiration, the knife strike leaving a gash in her stomach, and I whispered that my provisions be brought to me, for I had a quarter of Tam's salve left within my pack, and I cursed that I had used the healing scrolls, never replenishing, made by clerics in the greater town and cities.

Orders were given to Gwynnru to fetch Flukaggrrr, and Flukaggrrr listened as I broke my word. The wildmen who had slain the goblins but nearly defeated me, were to be stripped and executed. I was in no mood to allow any in their party to join with Patroal Irlaneson.

Initially they had been lined up with only a dagger each, and a few provisions, ready to depart, for there is a fine balance between honouring your word and precipitating hatred, but seeing Hilda's dreadful condition, fury overthrew my mind. I thought of sparing one and sending him away, a warning to others. I didn't, all died.

Later I walked back to the tower, leaving Hilda in the care of the women, the effects of the magical dart wearing away. The town was secure, no one leaving. There a debt to pay and the gates were still serviceable. The townsfolk receiving their freedom would now be subject and stripped of all their wealth. This battle was different, and they owed me, as I did my men.

Hilda survived although it took a week before she spoke to me again; one of her friends had died taking some of the blows that Patroal Irlaneson had aimed at her. She didn't miscarry but for a while it was considered likely.

I was an idiot, having failed to comprehend the strength of my enemy, failed to replenish at my own expense the healing scrolls that could have helped Hilda, and failed in the swift victory promised to my men.

My fury burning white hot, Patroal Irlaneson might think his escape secure, but I wouldn't allow him to travel far.

The world's a place of bastards, blood and slaughter, and I wasn't disproving anything. This time I'd do better.

*

Patroal Irlaneson ran with a knife in his hand, his heart labouring, his weak muscles being pushed to their limits, for fear of death gives energy to the body, allowing the stag to flee the hounds. And so it was that never having run since he was a child, he fled down the rear of the hill, tumbling, twisting his ankle but giving no heed, heading for the trees, not stopping.

Such was the desperation of his hour, the panic forcing sinew, knowing that he would be pursued, he ran blindly on, hoping he had killed the witch. *A lesson to the upstart lord. If only that cow of a servant hadn't gotten in the way.* Still, he hoped he'd done enough.

*

Gwynnru and two men stood guard as I lay on the ground in the basement of the old windmill, Hjalmar's former tower, and Gwynnru knew I wasn't dead.

In meditation, not sitting but lying as it eased the pain in my back – still slightly bleeding, but of no consequence. Wisp and I descended into the earth song, passing the ocean of altered perceptions, seeking the most powerful of my craft, the ability to port myself.

The rhapsody of the earth song is beautiful and soothing, but today there was no harmony sufficient to distract the fire within my heart.

Wisp assisted in gathering the strands of connective energy, done so many times before, but this time his mental acuity would be needed to reinforce my own, for I wanted to gather as much as my mind could cope with. Wisp would reinforce, helping, taking onboard some of the discomfort.

Eventually, not sure of time, I brought my mind back, the pang of leaving this oasis of peace registering upon my thoughts. Passing once more across the ocean of altered perceptions, colours speeding below, coming to wakefulness I opened my eyes, sitting up. "How long have I lain on the floor, Gwynnru?"

"Less than a quarter of the hour, Lord." And he asked needlessly, "Are you alright?"

"Fine." As I drew my sword, the men stepped back, not sure why I would draw it amongst allies, not understanding my motivation.

Twitching, the sword pointed north-northwest, and Wisp flew ahead, for I had no idea of distance.

"You can come as well if you like, Gwynnru?"

"I'll go wherever you command." And he hadn't realised – why would he? – that I intended to 'port', grasping his hand, I knew not where.

"As before to this tower, you and I." And I watched sympathetic to Gwynnru as he baulked, coming to a slow realisation that this was going to involve craft – the 'demon craft', as he liked to call it, though he said it not to me.

*

Gwynnru walked into the hall, followed by Flukaggrrr.

"Sod off, Gwynnru. I'm discussing whether you were worth saving, whether you'll die!"

"Lord?" He looked at Flukaggrrr.

He's writing about us, whether you died or not.

"Whether I died? But I'm here… now!"

"Apparently so. So it seems you didn't die! He's got these scribes on the floor, scribbling notes about his heroism, looking to write down his history!" And he smiled as a thought came into his head. *Don't forget to write about your incompetence, Lord. That'll be quite a few chapters.*

"Fuck off, Flukaggrrr, or I might write about the time you fornicated with that cow."

"Very funny, Lord." Smiling, he added, "It wasn't me but Gwynnru!"

And Gwynnru really didn't get it.

"Lord?!" spoke Gwynnru.

*

I really liked Gwynnru; he was competent with a sword, relying as I did on intuition, never needing to think too hard. His loyalty was without question.

But the best? The best was... he wasn't intelligent enough to formulate a plan of treachery. It made him the finest 'captain' of my guard – not thick, not an imbecile, but content in his duty.

He really wasn't as stupid as I portrayed. Thick, yes, but sometimes he surprised me. To describe him accurately would be 'a man who chose not to challenge his brain, though he could if need warranted, rise to the challenge'... perfect!

And back in the old windmill, Hjalmar's tower, he looked at the floor where I had lain. "If my lord wants me, I shall be glad." Yet his words spoke of a fear that was understandable.

"Yes, I want it." I was not actually sure I did, but Gwynnru might as well get used to the experience.

I sighed to myself. Did I push him too far?

*

Patroal Irlaneson, bruised, for he had fallen a few times, his cloak hindering his progress, catching upon brambles and branches as he ran and now bundled under his arm, having the wits not to discard it, started to relax.

His ankle hurt, thorns had cut into his hands and arms, but slowing down, breathing heavily he tried to listen. No sound, no baying of hounds.

"Sodding Hell!" He reached, looking for his purse, hoping against hope that it hadn't been taken from him. It had.

At least I'm free and that bastard half-orc will suffer. That's, as soon as I can rejoin with Edric. And shaking, the strength given through flight coursing through his veins, he reached within his pocket, lifting a seam, and extracted three small gems – not expensive, but a hidden wealth that would be used to provide payment for services.

He wanted to reach the coast, find a sailing vessel and try to rejoin with Edric or some of his brethren in faith, and he winced at the thought of his slain 'brothers'.

*

Wisp returned half an hour later, having located our quarry some seven miles from Isthmi. *He's very flustered, I don't think he likes you at all!'*

'Excellent! He'll like me even less when I've gutted him.' And with my back still aching – it had stopped bleeding, but there would be more blood on my clothes shortly – and taking Gwynnru's hand, he no longer distracted by the perils of battle having had time to contemplate the 'demon magic', trembled slightly. My guttural words, twisted vocal sounds as my spell was actioned, didn't allay his anxiety, and as two other soldiers, my men, witnessed, Gwynnru and I vanished.

It took a further action of craft, before I with Wisp's guidance placed myself fifty yards in front of Patroal Irlaneson's position.

Gwynnru knew that only I would be allowed to kill him, so as he ran terrified, like a rabbit chased by a hound, I watched Gwynnru trip him, the courtier falling into a bramble bush, and as I approached, he despite the thorns tried to bury himself in the matt of cutting, tearing spikes, hoping without hope that this might prolong his life a little.

I wish I'd brought some oil, a large bladderful, for I would have set fire to the bush, roasting him a little. As it was, I cut at the thicket until grabbing a leg, he was dragged out, pissing himself and laying prostrate at my feet.

Leaning down I hamstrung both his legs, cut off his genitals, stuck them down his throat and started to gut him slowly, pulling out his intestines as he watched still alive, screaming.

I was so glad he didn't faint, for the blood of my father's orcish heart was given full rein; cruelty unleashed, no restraint, no mercy.